The Beast of Eridu
Terran Strike Marines book 4

By

Richard Fox

&

Scott Moon

Copyright © 2018 Richard Fox & Scott Moon

All rights reserved.

ISBN: 9781790394272

heavy strap over it. "You think bitching at the ghost of Chesty Puller is going to make this drop go any easier? Don't hear Opal complaining. Right, Opie?"

"Kill Kesaht." The doughboy's grip on the metal ring tightened, bending it ever so slightly.

"Someone gets it," Duke said, touching the stock of his sniper rifle jutting over his shoulder.

Through the small windows in the side of the dropship, light diffused through nighttime clouds as fires raged below and explosions flashed up and against the cloud cover.

"Bombardment looks light," Hoffman said as he swiped through data feeds. "And we're losing telemetry from the rest of the assault force. As expected."

"We figure out how the Kesaht keep scrambling comms, I'll feel a lot more useful," Max said. "I signed up to be more than a bullet tosser and a bullet catcher."

"Yeah, if you could avoid the latter, I'd appreciate

it," Booker said. "Though I wonder if you got shot on Koensuu just to miss out on all the cold."

"I'm still shivering from that ice ball," Garrison said.

Hoffman looked over one shoulder, down his line of Strike Marines. One, the shortest, hadn't spoken. The Dotari was normally close-lipped—or close-beaked in the alien's case—before an operation. Dotari military culture believed that pre-deployment discussion meant the plan was flawed.

Red warning lights flashed through the dropship.

"Two minutes." King flicked a switch on his gauss rifle and the weapon's magnetic fields powered on. "Lock and load. Remember your sectors when we drop. Violence of action. Check your buddy."

Hoffman tugged on his handle then touched the gauss magazines and grenades mag-locked to his power armor. He turned to Max and checked a small screen incorporated into the man's shoulder pauldron. Max's power levels and suit integrity read green. He gave the commo Marine a slap on his shoulder.

"You're ready to rock and roll," the lieutenant said.

"You're good, sir," Max replied and bumped a fist against Hoffman's arm.

"Hey! Watch it, buddy," Duke said, slapping away Gor'al's hand.

"It is unsecured!" The Dotari Marine reached for a pouch on the sniper's hip.

"The hell it is!" Duke slapped away Gor'al's hand. "You want to keep those fingers? Keep your mitts off my chewing tobacco."

"But if you're a casualty, then—"

"You still can't have my dip!"

"Look alive! Release in five!" the pilot shouted through the ship's intercom.

The Mule dipped down and accelerated, then nosed

up. The maneuver dragged on Hoffman's stomach and he had to pull against the handle and push up from the trap door to keep his balance.

The door snapped open and Hoffman fell into hell. Lines of fire burned across a steppe, barren but for grass and the crisscross snap of gauss tracers and energy blasts. The line of spun titanium connecting the handle to the Mule caught and lowered him toward the ground.

A bolt of blue fire streaked past him and impacted the bottom of the Mule. He felt the ship wobble through the line.

"Release! Release!" Hoffman let go and fell, accelerating toward a small fire. In his armor, he weighed close to three hundred pounds and was not about to land gently. He put his feet and knees together just before he hit, rolling with his momentum through flames.

Ignoring the heat building through his boots, he quickly orientated himself to the battlefield. The Mule shot away, blowing dust and embers across his visor.

"Team, sound off!" Hoffman went prone in a patch of dirt that wasn't on fire and tried to contact headquarters as gunfire thundered around him.

"We're good to go." King shot a thumbs-up to Hoffman.

"Team, move to waypoint Alpha One," Hoffman said, rising to a low crouch and rushing toward a marker on his HUD. He scanned the tundra through the synergistic optics of his helmet and gauss rifle as feeds from Duke and Max illuminated a corner of his heads-up display.

He relaxed. He was made for this. There wasn't time to worry about politics or personalities. This was go time. Commanding Marines in the middle of chaos was what he was trained for and what his team needed from him right now.

"I would not steal from you if you were not a stingy human," Gor'al moaned as he covered Duke's flank.

"Stow that noise," King ordered.

"Phase two," Hoffman said, "find the bunkers!"

Eagle air-support fighters ripped over the battlefield, engines distorting sound for miles in every direction. Missiles jumped from their short wings and streaked over a low ridge in the distance.

"Those were maverick missiles," Garrison said. "That means Kesaht tanks are coming."

"Maybe the missiles blew up all the tanks," Booker said.

"You want to be out here in the open flapping when a tank comes over that ridge?" Garrison's head whipped from side to side, taking in the open terrain. "Bad place to be!"

Energy bolts blasted out the ground at the base of the ridge and the team dove to the ground.

"Found the bunker!" Max shouted.

"Not a lot of cover around here," Duke complained

as he flopped down on the highest elevation in the area—an anemic escarpment about six feet high—and pulled his sniper kit forward. Gor'al went prone beside him, aiming his weapon at the bunkers that looked a lot closer and more dangerous with crew-served weapons pointing out of the slots.

At another point on their firing line, Booker handed Garrison grenades for the launcher slung under the barrel of his gauss rifle.

"Frag out," Garrison said, firing once, twice, and a third time as Booker struggled to keep up. Explosions blasted against the bunker but failed to enter the small firing ports.

"Move position," Hoffman directed via the infrared lasers connecting their helmets.

"Moving," Garrison said.

"Covering," Max answered.

Duke and Gor'al followed a similar routine. "Two

bunkers sighted and marked. Moving to the next redoubt."

Kesaht gunners sprayed tracer rounds into the night, where they skipped across the frozen steppes.

Hoffman watched his team from behind Opal while the doughboy placed careful shots in another window slot of the bunker.

"Command to Hammer Six, have you neutralized your targets?" The landing commander's voice rang in Hoffman's ears, nearly crystal clear.

"Waiting on a response," Hoffman answered. "Duke, hold overwatch. Don't lose your assistant this time."

"I never lost him."

"I was on a side mission," Gor'al said.

"Not the time right now. Get to work," Hoffman said. He checked his people and moved, steering Opal by the back of his armor. The doughboy formed a moving body bunker that was reassuring.

"We're set," Gor'al said. "I am thinking my partner will share a dip since I carried so much of his gear."

"Clear the air, Gor'al," Duke said. "Ice Claw for Hammer Six, the horses are on the move."

The thrill of fear raced up Hoffman's spine. "Understood. Max, get me Command."

Sanheel shock troops, centaur-like aliens that stood nearly eight feet tall, charged over the ridgeline, galloping far faster than a human could ever run.

"Go for Command," Max said an instant later.

The ground rumbled as dirt and ice exploded into the morning dawn behind the charge.

"Hammer Six to Command, we've got a pony counterattack." Hoffman cut the transmission without waiting for a confirmation. The boss could wait while he dealt with a deadly threat. "Let's hit 'em, Hammers!"

"Kill enemy!" Opal roared, shifting his fire to the charging Sanheel.

"These bunkers are still making noise!" Garrison shouted.

"Then shut them up!" Hoffman yelled.

"Sir need to move!" Opal yelled, dragging Hoffman to a better position.

Garrison fired the last of his grenades and switched straight to full auto with his gauss rifle. "Get some!"

Hoffman let the violation pass. He felt his own adrenaline surge as he marched his rounds into the charging enemy. One of the officers outpaced the others, so Hoffman cut his legs from under him and watched several tons of Sanheel plow into the ground.

His Strike Marines opened up with their gauss rifles, sending up a wall of magnetically driven bolts that smashed into the charging foe. Hoffman felt the still ground, at odds with the sight of the thundering hooves, and braced his rifle against his shoulder as he emptied another magazine.

He swiveled toward another target just as a message flashed across his HUD.

SIMULATION TERMINATED

The Sanheel vanished and fire from the bunkers cut off. To the team's left and right, the snap of gauss rifles carried over the battlefield.

"What the actual hell?" Duke sat up on his knees.

Opal beat a meaty fist against his heavy gauss cannon, the barrel glowing hot. "Opal break again!"

"No! No! No!" Garrison shouted. "I was just starting to enjoy this. Opal, what'd you do?"

"It's not him, Garrison. Simulation's over. Recover," King said.

Hoffman slapped a new magazine into his rifle but got an error message on his HUD. His weapon had been disabled and wouldn't cycle a bullet into the chamber.

"Gor'al, did you make *another* safety violation?" Max asked.

"You mean did you remember not to maneuver in front of my line of fire while I was providing overwatch?" The snap of the Dotari's beak cut through the air.

New orders popped up on Hoffman's visor. His lip twitched as he scanned over the text.

"Stop grumbling and bring it in," Hoffman said. "There's a Mule coming to pick us up. Gunney, see the team's weapons readied safe for transport."

"That was a textbook-perfect landing and deployment," Max said. "How many times are we going to do this?"

"Until we can't get it wrong," King said.

Max shook his head, fatigue evident on his face.

It took Hoffman a second to understand what Max was complaining about. "Sim didn't get cancelled for the way we did the drop."

Max touched a panel on his gauntlet screen and an antenna extended up from the radio pack on his back.

"We're cut off from all the comm networks," Max said. "Sir?"

"I don't know anything more than we need to get on the bird that's coming for us." Hoffman's shoulders slumped ever so slightly.

"Your instructions mention the three-day pass we're supposed to get after this training evolution, sir?" Max stretched out the last word, blatantly fishing for more information.

"They did not," Hoffman said as he watched a Mule crest over the horizon. His team spread out into a circle, weapons oriented out, as they waited for pickup.

"You wanted guaranteed time off, you should've joined the Sky Watch," King said. "Strike Marines are mission first…people always."

"Recruiter lied to me." Max shook his head.

"Hey, me too." Garrison pushed his visor up and took a bite of beef jerky. "Said Strike Marines did orbital landings all the time. Never had to walk anywhere."

"Mine said I'd be up to my neck in ladies." Duke tucked a pinch of chewing tobacco into his lip then slapped away Gor'al's hand. "He wasn't wrong."

"They just want the singles you tuck into their G-strings," Garrison said.

"That don't make him wrong. Just makes me broke." Duke spat into the dirt.

The Mule swooped low, landing fast without evasive combat maneuvers. As every member of the team hustled toward the open ramp, a crewman directed them to a bench.

Garrison clamped one hand on Max's shoulder as the two sat down. "We can't keep doing this over just for you. If you don't start showing improvement, we'll need to draw a replacement from the Dotari Marines."

Gor'al nodded excitedly. "That is an outstanding idea! I have many friends who are Dotari!"

"I didn't see that coming," Booker said, removing her helmet and reaching back to adjust her tight bun of hair.

Hoffman climbed into the Mule and stowed his gear along the wall, the promised three-day pass on his mind. His Hammers had been training hard for weeks against Kesaht targets, prepping for an operation that they still didn't have the details for. The next big push against the Kesaht was being planned far above his pay grade, but he had sources. As much as good training was the best form of welfare for his Marines, they still needed to blow off steam from time to time.

Hoffman strapped into the bench as the Mule angled up and accelerated. He felt the rumble through the deck plates and checked the angle of ascent through the window. They were burning for orbit.

Gunney King sat next to him. "Anything?"

"No, just get on the Mule." Hoffman touched his gauntlet screen then tapped King's, transferring the order to the senior NCO.

"I got a bad feeling about this," King said. "Getting yanked out of the middle of a training exercise like that? Bet the brass had kittens over that move."

"And our comms are off-line...could be good news," Hoffman said.

"You think they're sending us after the *Breitenfeld*?" King asked. The Ibarra Nation had captured the ship and her entire crew, including the war hero Admiral Valdar, during the battle over Syracuse. Hoffman and his team had been walking through the planet's deserts, trying to get back to the fight, when they learned what happened to their ship.

In the weeks that followed, there had been no trace of the *Breitenfeld* or the critical Keystone jump-gate technology she'd carried. Hoffman and his team were reassigned to the Second Assault Corps and thrown into the line for training.

"We've been jerked around too much lately," Hoffman said, looking over his team. They were all exhausted. "No need to get hopes up just yet."

"Damn Ibarrans," King said. "Terran Union's been fighting losing battles against the Kesaht in a dozen systems. They pop up to gank the *Breit* from us then vanish. You'd think they'd want to fight the Kesaht too."

"Least we're not fighting the Ibarra Nation *and* the Kesaht," Hoffman said. "Yet."

"Yet," King said. "I don't care how many Ibarrans are in our way. We're getting the *Breitenfeld* back."

"From your lips to God's ears," Hoffman said.

A voice crackled over the intercom. "This is your highly professional and talented pilot speaking. Stand by for afterburners."

The Mule jumped skyward, squashing them into their seats and shaking them with each course correction.

"I thought the training scenario was over," Max

said.

"Stop being such a girl, Max," Garrison said.

Booker punched Garrison under the arm, right where his armor was weakest.

"Ouch! I've got to cover that opening around you. So many nerves in the armpit."

Booker took another shot with the other hand, flattening her fist into more of a wedge for greater penetration. Garrison twisted his body at the same time he attempted to deflect the strike with the palm of his hand. The result was partially successful.

"That's enough," King said. "Fight decision goes to Booker."

"Which makes her thirty and one against you." Max ducked a swing from Garrison.

King leaned close to Hoffman. "I hate to say this, LT, but I think we need to get them on a real mission before someone gets hurt."

Hoffman smiled.

King returned the gesture with a bit of a laugh. "I'm not sure why, but it's almost like we're having a good time out here."

"Training's a lot more fun than actually getting shot at. I just had one of those feelings, you know? Like we're family." King made a manly grunt.

"Don't get all soft and sentimental on me, Gunney. You know this is going to get ugly. Like boarding an alien ghost ship and fighting the last remaining Xaros or encountering a new race of galactic conquerors on an ice world as we get betrayed by spies."

"Please stand by for docking protocols," the pilot said. "The Mule will be locked down until we're contacted by…some sort of VIP. Who the hell are you jarheads?"

"We're Valdar's Hammer!" Max yelled toward the cockpit. "That flyboy just call us jarheads? To our face?"

Everyone on the team, including Opal, looked

toward Hoffman. The mood went from jovial to grim in a split second. They were locked inside unless Garrison had some unauthorized denethrite in his pocket, which he didn't.

"I can't stand pilots without a sense of humor," Garrison said. "Why the hell are we getting locked in this fart box?"

"Black ops. Intel corps. I could care less about his sense of humor, but I don't like being put in a holding pattern for no reason. Something's not right," Hoffman said.

A few minutes later, the Mule entered the docking bay of a corvette-class starship, the *Scipio*, and settled to the deck. A few minutes after that, the ramp lowered and a man wearing a plain naval uniform stepped through. Average height, bland face, and a trim but not excessively fit physique made him completely forgettable.

Max cursed and twisted away from the man. "Not

this asshole again!" He started to come out of his chair, but Garrison held him down.

****

"Lieutenant Hoffman, I've been authorized to compliment your proficiency on the recently completed training cycle. Very satisfactory," said Commander Kutcher of Naval Intelligence before he hurried to say, "Your team's been reassigned—"

Hoffman stood between the man and his team. "Get to the point, sir. We going after Valdar or our ship?"

"No." Kutcher's jaw worked from side to side. "President Garret has ordered all efforts against the Ibarrans to cease, at least until we've regained operational momentum against the Kesaht and their allies."

"He's abandoning the *Breitenfeld*?" Hoffman asked. "And Valdar? They won the Ember War. Humanity would be extinct without him or that ship."

"The Dotari would be extinct twice without Valdar," Gor'al said, waving a fist in the air. "Once because of these nice Marines here. Thank you for curing the phage."

"Stop. Thanking. Us," King said through clenched teeth.

"The *Breitenfeld* and her crew are not a priority for the Terran Union," Kutcher said. "Not right now. Your team was a by-name request for a critical mission."

"The *Breitenfeld* is critical. The war against the Kesaht is critical," Hoffman said. "Why aren't we back preparing for…whatever mission's coming up?"

"Maybe you don't want to be on that Hail Mary." The intelligence officer's face darkened.

Hoffman held up a hand for him to stop. "The Kesaht are the real threat. Don't give me politics and espionage. We're on mission and can't be taken off without the highest authority. What could be more important than Kesaht forces slaughtering entire populations and stealing children?"

Kutcher bored his beady eyes into Hoffman. Ship parts ticked as they changed temperature from the flight.

"I'm only going to say this once, Lieutenant Hoffman," Kutcher said. "Your new assignment is part of the larger war effort. Your feelings on the matter are irrelevant. You are to take your team to Nimrod II and recruit a tech advisor."

"I'm the tech advisor!" Gor'al burst out.

Kutcher glared at the Dotari for a moment. "Then, you, Lieutenant Hoffman, will take that tech advisor and link up with Colonel Fallon on Eridu for further instructions."

"Why so vague?" Hoffman asked. "Who's this tech advisor? Why do you need him or her on Eridu? Eridu…why haven't I heard of that place before?"

"A sensitive human population was resettled there after the Ember War," Kutcher said. "They've been engaged in critical research ever since and colonization was restricted. The entire planet is a black site due to archaeotech research, and it is within range of a Kesaht attack from the Crucible gate the enemy just seized on Boralis III. Fallon and his ad hoc unit were sent to help with the evacuation after the fight on Syracuse. A situation has developed and he requested you to deal with it."

"Fallon asked for me…" Hoffman trailed off. The colonel was the uncle of a fallen Marine, one with whom Hoffman had a history.

"We're stretched thin with the war effort," Kutcher said. "You'll have no backup on Nimrod or Eridu. Now get off this shuttle. It's taking me back to Earth. Your mission specifics," said the intelligence officer as he tossed a data stick to Hoffman, then jerked a thumb over his shoulder to the *Scipio's* cargo bay. "Move it."

Hoffman stood, tilted his head toward the ramp, and walked off the Mule, his team behind him.

"I don't like that guy," Max said.

"Stand by for Mule launch," the pilot announced after barely enough time had passed for Kutcher to disembark. "On behalf of myself and the flight crew, we do apologize for any inconvenience the lack of a layover has caused each and every one of my valued passengers…"

Hoffman released his breath.

"Lame, but he's trying. Max, go up there and school this flyboy on his jokes," Garrison said.

Hoffman snapped the data stick into his gauntlet and read over the new orders. King flagged down a petty officer, who looked shocked to see dirty, angry Strike Marines on his ship.

Booker leaned toward Hoffman. "Are we going to miss the big show?"

"Are we a bunch of spy chasers again?" Duke

asked.

"No. Bodyguards is more like it," Hoffman said and sent the orders to his team.

"What is a Karigole?" Gor'al asked as the Dotari removed his helmet. The alien swung the thick black quills on his scalp from side to side and sweat sprinkled out onto the deck. A flat nose flared just over a blunt beak. Hoffman was tempted to compare the alien to a Rastafarian parakeet but would never do so out loud.

"They're a special race of technical advisors, much better than Dotari in most things," Duke said.

"Yeah, they're smarter and better-looking than Dotari," Garrison said, jumping in. "Better manners."

"They never steal dip," Duke said.

"And their fashion sense is sharper," Booker added.

Gor'al spread his hands defensively. "This isn't my armor! You made me wear this. It belongs to a human woman. You force me to wear it because you humans don't have the discipline to avoid shooting something that isn't dressed exactly like you."

"There's no difference," Booker said.

"Gor'al did not mean to offend you, Sergeant Booker. These words are not what I meant. But look at me," he said, waving his hands over his gear.

"And?" Booker said.

"You look great," Duke said, slapping him on the leg. "I was just kidding about the Karigole. Haven't you seen that movie *Last Stand on Takeni*? There was a Karigole in that. Steuben, right?"

"Oh, t*hose* Karigole," Gor'al said. "I did not know they were still a thing. First, I serve aboard the *Breitenfeld,* then I meet one of my race's saviors. I will be like Duke when I return home. Up to my neck in—how does he say it?—up to my neck in pu—"

Duke slapped a hand over Gor'al's beak, his head shaking from side to side.

"Steuben is who we're supposed to recruit off Nimrod," Hoffman said. "Which I doubt will be easy, given what this file says about the Karigole. They were granted a colony under a Terran Union protectorate right after the Ember War, but they broke off all communication with us a few years ago. Phoenix sent a representative to talk to them, but the mission was called off…after the Karigole shot arrows at the contact team. Minor injuries."

"So we've got to recruit this Karigole and they've got a 'no trespassers' sign out?" King asked. "Recruit him for what?"

"I don't have that in the mission brief," Hoffman said.

Garrison tossed his hands up. "Just another day in the Strike Marines," the breacher said. "What's the name of this ship? The *Skippy?* Where's the head and where's the chow hall? Might as well enjoy this brief pause while we can."

"First we clean weapons." King leveled a knife hand at Garrison's chest. "Then we clean gear. Then we secure a berthing. Then we report to the chief of the boat for taskings. Then, maybe, we can worry about ourselves."

"I'll leave you to it, Gunney," Hoffman said. "I'm going to find the captain. Somebody on this ship might have some more answers."

Chapter 2

The *Scipio's* command center boasted a few workstations and a captain's chair, but it was cramped compared to the relative spaciousness Hoffman remembered aboard the *Breitenfeld*'s bridge. Holo panels on the bulkheads created faux windows to either side of the forward view ports. Hoffman stood to one side of the captain's chair—an old, beat-up unit. He saw it as just another room with too many computers and view screens. His place was off to one side in a roughly human-sized, recessed part of the wall where he was expected to strap himself in if they saw action. Navy types preferred their Marine cargo to stay out of the way most of the time. He gripped a railing, looking like a sore thumb in his bulky power armor compared to the sailors in their slimmer void suits.

The *Scipio*'s master and commander, Lieutenant Commander Tagawa leaned forward in her chair and frowned at the tan planet beyond the basalt spikes of the Crucible gate surrounding the ship.

"Sensors, give me an update," she said.

"System reads dead," a petty officer called out from a workstation.

"'Identify Friend or Foe' pings keep hitting us," another sailor said. "We're getting painted by out-system macro cannons, orbital torpedo magazines, and ground-based rail cannons. It's all automated…which does not give me a warm and fuzzy."

"Welcome to Nimrod, everyone," Tagawa said. "The Karigole want us to see the 'No Soliciting' sign. Least they haven't changed the targeting computers to blow any arrivals out of space. We should still be able to knock on the front door. Or at least our Strike Marines will."

"I'm sure that will go just fine," Hoffman deadpanned. "Do we know why the Karigole became so unfriendly? They worked well with us during the Ember War. Valdar and the *Breitenfeld* got the last of their species off that Toth planet, Nibiru."

"That secret-squirrel type that met you in my cargo bay didn't say," the captain said. "Not sure if he didn't know or we didn't have the need to know. You know how spies are."

"I don't need to know why the Karigole shot the last human they saw in the buttocks with an arrow?" Hoffman asked.

"Don't look at me." She shrugged. "Get your away-team ready. None of you wear red shirts under your power armor, do you?"

"Why would that matter?"

"Philistine." She rolled her eyes. "There's one

landing pad on the planet. The automated defenses are rather clear that we'll be fired upon if we set down anywhere but that landing pad, so be prepared to do some walking. The Karigole settlement is several miles from where we'll touch down."

She tossed a small data drive to the Marine.

"There's your full mission brief," she said. "I had to wait until we made transit to give it to you. Everything with planet Eridu is classified. Just another pain in the ass we can thank Kutcher for."

"Roger." Hoffman connected the drive to his gauntlet. "I'll be in the cargo bay, ready to disembark."

"I'll remind you there's no backup," she said. "You Strike Marines get into trouble, don't think my sailors are going to be much help outside this ship."

"Noted." Hoffman gave her a salute she didn't return and left the bridge.

Chapter 3

Hoffman moved quickly through the short, narrow hallways of the *Scipio*, ducking around bulkheads and dodging sailors that moved with a sense of purpose. The partial conversations and constant bustling noise of the ship reminded him there was more to the war effort than just his Strike Marines and their constant missions.

The ship jumped under his feet at the first touch of the planet's atmosphere. Compared to a combat drop, this was a walk in the park. It'd been a while since he deployed on anything but a Mule.

In the deployment bay, he found his team waiting

and ready. "King, give me a PCI. I've been in officer country. Feeling un-squared away."

"Right away, sir." The NCO performed a quick, thorough check of Hoffman's armor. "Looks good, sir."

"Strap in. The *Scipio*'s putting us down on Nimrod. The landing zone's in the middle of a savanna," said Hoffman as the ship slipped deeper into the atmosphere without the teeth-clattering turbulence of a Mule landing.

"I could get used to this," Garrison said.

"A fat plug of dip would make it better," Gor'al said.

Duke grunted, his bottom lip packed with chewing tobacco.

The team shifted uneasily as they watched clouds streak past portholes. Garrison opened the breach on the grenade launcher attached to his gauss rifle, then touched an ammo pouch.

"We going in hot?" he asked.

"Karigole are allies of the Terran Union," Hoffman said. "There aren't many of them, but they made a real difference during the Ember War. We're here to talk to the one named Steuben—not get into a fight."

"They know that?" Max asked.

"The Karigole live in a low-tech environment," Hoffman said. "Bows and arrows. Spears. Nothing that can get through our armor." He touched his breastplate. "Everyone stay frosty down there. Frosty and sharp."

"Don't humans have a saying about never meeting your heroes?" Gor'al asked. "Is there an addendum about never shooting those same heroes? But if you meet a Buddha on the road, then why should you kill him?"

"Gor'al, what did I tell you about studying human religion?" King asked.

"That humans have been trying to find those answers for thousands of years without luck and I shouldn't try either?" the Dotari said.

"Yes. That," King said.

The ship set down with a jolt through the landing struts and warning lights flashed around the ramp as it lowered. Sunset shone through the opening and a gust of hot, dry air hit Hoffman's face. He put his helmet on and made his way down the ramp, careful to keep his rifle pointed low and not up at the ready as his training and instincts demanded.

Hoffman and his team moved down the deployment ramp, gazing across starkly beautiful grasslands. The landing pad was a square slab that looked large enough to fit two or three more corvettes. Grass encroached on the edge of the concrete. No buildings. No sign of civilization.

"*Scipio Actual for Hammer Six, what's your status?*" Tagawa asked over the IR.

Hoffman swept his eyes over the terrain. "Negative on a welcoming party. Any contact with the locals via radio?"

"Nothing. Though the automated defenses just informed me we have ten minutes of ground time before we're declared hostile. I'm not going to argue with programming. As such, we need to get back into orbit. Plcase move clear of the launch zone."

Hoffman signaled his team with a knife hand. "Patrol formation. Move out."

The moment they were over the next rise, the *Scipio* blasted off and swerved away from them.

"It's not like they were going to be much help anyway," King said.

"The settlement's eight miles to the east," Hoffman said. "Keep your eyes peeled. I have a feeling we're already being watched."

Chapter 4

Hoffman and King separated, each taking half the team as they moved into the scrublands where patches of tall grass thrust up through gravel and dried mud. A series of mesas shadowed the horizon to the west while north and east were mountain foothills.

"Watch your spacing," Hoffman broadcast over the squad link.

King clicked his mic twice.

"Let's stretch our legs a bit," Hoffman said as they started to double-time it. With pseudo-muscle-enhanced armor, they made outstanding time. "Look for defensible ground, get oriented, and see about finding the Karigole."

Hoffman set an aggressive pace and his team kept up and looked after each other. Opal ran near him, his boots slamming the rough soil like jackhammers.

"We better slow down, LT. Opal isn't made for long distances," Max complained.

"Funny, I don't hear him complaining," Hoffman said then did a double take. "King, did you see what I saw?"

"Movement to our left flank. Someone or something paralleling us."

Hoffman took his team to a slight rise around a large rock formation. The sandy prairie stretched down and away in every direction. "Duke, tell me what you see."

"On it," Duke said. "Opal, give me a boost."

The doughboy pressed the sniper above his head. Seconds later, the sniper scrambled onto the top of the rock and went prone with his optics.

Wind and swaying grass passed the time.

"Whoever or whatever you fine gentlemen think you saw is gone," Duke said. "Or it was your imagination. Don't even see a residual heat pass on the ground."

Hoffman didn't argue.

"If Duke didn't see it, it wasn't there," Booker said.

"That's the nicest thing you've ever said to me, Doc." The sniper paused. "Look there, two-forty degrees at three hundred meters."

Hoffman trained his optics on a herd of bright orange gazelle-analogs nearly lost in the rising sun. Ordinarily, he'd be skeptical of their camouflage, but in this light, they were almost invisible.

"They're on the move. Probably traveling to a watering hole with large numbers of other herbivores to shelter from predators, but they timed it poorly." Duke's voice was quiet, reverent as a big-game hunter seeing new prey for the first time.

"Shit," Max said.

Hoffman's gut tightened as three blurs of yellow and orange shot from a line of scrub and ran down the slowest of the orange and brown gazelles.

"Hot damn! Those things have big teeth," Duke said. "Straight-up sabretooths. Somebody's cubs are eating meat tonight."

"There'll be other predators. Can't tell if we smell like dinner or not to them," Hoffman said.

"Maybe our Karigole hosts will give us some useful survival tips," Max said, looking around theatrically. "Wait, they're not here."

Garrison slapped him on the back of his helmet. "Hey, you act like you've gone poking around a ship that was supposed to be full of friendly aliens, only to be chased around by inhuman monsters that want to rip your arms off."

"Once bitten, twice shy," Max said.

"I will not turn into a banshee," Gor'al said. "I promise."

Hoffman sent a message to the *Scipio*: "No sign of hosts. Charlie Mike." Continue Mission.

Birds circled something beyond the horizon. The roar of stalkers echoed from the kill site as they ate. A large, angry hawk creature screeched.

"Just in time for dinner," Booker said.

Shadows grew long as the sun slipped below the horizon.

Hoffman motioned King into a conference. "This isn't the worst position from a tactical perspective—good field of view, some cover in the rocks, but no water or other sustainables. I'd rather not try and approach the settlement during hours of darkness. That might spook the Karigole."

"This mission isn't as time sensitive," King said. "We can afford to wait until morning."

"Good. Let's move out in five. See if Opal can get

Duke down from his perch without hurting him," Hoffman said.

His team watched three more kills and came close enough to make their own with gauss rifles if they'd had the need. Once Duke found a good campsite, Hoffman ordered them to eat, drink water, and sleep in shifts.

Duke pulled Hoffman aside. "Let me take one gazelle. That's all I ask. I could be back in an hour or two. I'm sure they'd taste great roasted over an open fire."

"We're not on safari or a walkabout."

Duke spat tobacco. "Had to try. For the record, the air is clear. I could take a two-thousand-meter shot."

"Of course."

****

Dawn broke six hours later. Hoffman wasn't sure if

the planet's axial tilt had the area in its summer season, or if Nimrod naturally rotated faster than Earth.

After silent reveille, less than five minutes passed before they were headed across the alien landscape—Duke on point, Garrison on the left flank, Booker on the right flank, and Opal bringing up the rear. Hoffman, King, Max, and Gor'al held the center of the travel formation but maintained distance from each other. They used helmet radios and hand signs to communicate. No two Strike Marines were close enough to be taken out by one grenade, rocket, or improvised device. The only exception was that Hoffman kept Max closer at hand because of his communications equipment.

Maneuvering across the open landscape was at once easier and more difficult. Team movements were simplified, but they were constantly exposed. They could have moved faster—he trained them hard on and off transport ships and on dozens of worlds—but they had no clear destination. The *Scipio* was on standby for pickup—a maneuver that took time that they probably wouldn't have if this was like their last mission or three.

"Just one gazelle," Duke said.

"Negative," Hoffman answered.

"I think the old man has something," Garrison chimed in. "What self-respecting officer doesn't have an orange gazelle head in their office? All clear on the left flank. Nothing seen, by the way."

"At what point did this turn into a Cub Scout nature walk?" King asked. "I may not be a runner like the lieutenant, but I will PT you until you hate me when we get home. I'm talking to you, Garrison."

Hoffman scanned the horizon and then worked his way closer, carefully manipulating his optic amplifiers in his helmet. "Those don't look like gazelle."

"You haven't seen the half of it," Duke said.

Just over the horizon were gazelle and other

creatures they had seen the day before. Hoffman and the rest of the team watched as a herd of elephant-sized creatures meandered to the watering hole. Their earth-colored hide and tufts of hair made them look like small hills had sprouted legs. Talons the size of Hoffman's arm extended from the creatures' feet and scraped the ground.

Hoffman checked his briefing map on his heads-up display and did a quick terrain orientation. They were approaching a small canyon that led to the Karigole settlement.

"I've got something," Duke said. "Need one of you to come up."

Hoffman signaled for King to stay with the main body of the team and jogged ahead. Impatience urged Hoffman forward and it took an effort of will not to sprint. Running would kick up dust, and even though he wanted the Karigole to know he was coming, his training still demanded he move tactically. He slowed as he approached the sniper, switched into a crouching advance, and crossed the final distance cautiously.

"There's some sort of blast zone here." Duke pointed at traces of debris. "I don't normally do this, but I'll admit something. I picked that up on my optic scanners before I saw it. Someone cleaned it up. Look closely. You'll see it's scorched."

"I see it." He ran his own field scan from his left gauntlet computer. "I think we're on the edge of the debris field."

He called up the rest of the team to search. Hoffman wanted to go look for himself but decided against it. The team was well-positioned and he didn't want to expose them by being careless. "King, I'm on overwatch. Take an element and scout out that area."

"On it," the Gunney sent back.

Hoffman and Duke watched as the other Strike Marines hurried toward the blackened area. One took a knee next to what looked like a jagged rock.

"*King for Hoffman,*" King said through the team's IR.

"Go for Hoffman."

"*There's a pretty good amount of metal here. No markings. Heat scored and warped. I'm collecting a sample for later. First guess is it was a ship that disintegrated on reentry.*"

"*Scipio* says we're the first ones through the Crucible in years," Hoffman said.

"*That so? Well, this grass was burnt not too long ago. No latent heat, but nature hasn't repaired the damage either,*" King said.

"That don't add up," Duke said.

"Maybe a defense satellite lost orbit," Hoffman said. "Or…something worse. Team," he said, switching to a wide-band channel so everyone could hear him, "we're pushing on the settlement. Form up on me."

****

Hoffman looked through the optics of his gauss rifle to the village on a small hilltop, laid out in concentric circles, with the door of every earthen hut facing toward a large building in the center. A wooden palisade around the perimeter was broken in several places. Thatch roofs looked intact, but he made out scorch marks on the walls. There'd been no sign of life since the team first got eyes on the location.

"Max, Booker, Garrison, with me." The lieutenant slid into a slight depression filled with shoulder-high grass. "Rest on overwatch."

"What do you think we'll find in there?" Garrison asked as he fell in a few steps to Hoffman's left.

"I hope we don't find anything," Hoffman said. "If the village has been wiped out, then we've got a more serious problem on our hands than Karigole that don't want to talk."

"Sir, look at this." Booker held up a wooden arrow, the shaft almost as long as her arm, the head a chipped bit of obsidian. "Big sucker. You know how strong you'd have to be to draw a bow back far enough to shoot this with a decent amount of force?"

"Karigole aren't small," Hoffman said.

"OK, I know our armor is graphenium composite and can take a full-power gauss shot and probably hold up," Garrison said, "but let's not get hit by any of those arrows either. Yeah?"

Booker turned the arrowhead over in the sunlight. "There's some sort of resin on here. Poison?"

"Oh fun," Max said. "Poison."

"My advice remains the same—don't get shot," Garrison said.

"So glad you're here, Marine," Hoffman said as he

moved toward the village at a crouch, his head just below the top of the grass.

Hoffman stopped at the edge of the field, a few dozen yards from the wooden barricades. He zoomed in on the singed walls and sent images back to the overwatch team.

"There's projectile damage," Duke said. "Gauss rounds. High-velocity hit passed straight through the walls. But that doesn't explain the blast marks…or the barricade damage. They look like a truck ran over them"

Garrison patted his rifle. "If the locals have bows and arrows, who's shooting the newer hardware?" he asked.

"Move in by twos," Hoffman said. "Keep tight."

The team emerged from the field and through a gap in the wooden barricade. Hoffman and Max went to one side of a house, Garrison and Booker the other. Hoffman quickly peeked around the side, then raised a hand next to his ear to signal for the team to move around opposite sides of the building.

He ducked beneath a diamond-shaped window and stopped next to the door that faced a much larger structure in the center of the village.

"Contact!" Garrison shouted through the IR. "No. Negative contact. Sir, you need to see what's to the ten o'clock of this structure."

"Coming around." Hoffman hustled over and found the other pair of Marines. Garrison had his rifle at his shoulder, pointed between other houses. Buried in rubble of a half-collapsed wall was a massive figure, its hooved legs sticking out from the packed earth. A long rifle of alien manufacture with a serrated bayonet was stuck into the ground next to the body.

"Shit." Hoffman hurried over to the corpse, checking corners along the way but seeing no one else. He kicked a hunk of wall off the body and a brutish tusked face stared up at him with dead eyes.

"It's a Sanheel," the lieutenant said. "The Kesaht got here first."

As he knelt closer to the centaur-like alien's body to take a quick temperature scan, he saw broken arrow shafts poking out of gaps in the alien's armor around the neck and shoulder.

"Body's at ambient temperature," Hoffman said. "Can't say how long it's been dead."

"This explains a lot." Garrison pointed to hoof marks in the ground and then toward open terrain to the east. "Ponies were here; at least a dozen, I'd say."

"But did they take all the Karigole?" Hoffman looked to the large building in the center of the village.

"Thirty-five houses," King said over the IR. "Assume three to four in each? No way a dozen Sanheel could carry that many."

"And there's no trace of the Karigole," Booker said.

"Raiders aren't known for burying the dead of those they can't carry off."

"So where'd Steuben and the others go?" Hoffman looked to the west, where mountains rose not too far off.

"Apaches hid from the American Army many years in the mountains of Cochise County," Gor'al said over the IR. *"Plenty of defensible terrain to the west."*

"How does the Dotari know this?" Garrison asked.

"Don't all of you study human military history? You all say 'Geronimo' when you do a parachute jump to honor the Apache leader. You mean you all don't know this?"

"Thank you, Gor'al," Hoffman said, resisting the urge to kick the dead Sanheel out of frustration. "We're going toward the mountains."

"What about the Kesaht?" King asked as he and the rest of the team entered the village.

"We're not here for them. We're here for Steuben.

The Crucible gate hasn't been active for years...but this bastard hasn't been dead that long. Can't even smell him through my helmet yet. The Kesaht are still on Nimrod."

"How'd they even get here if the gate's been offline?" Max asked.

"We'll find the Kesaht later," Hoffman said. "See if they'll tell us. Let's go."

****

Hoffman rotated King to point as they pressed into the narrow valley.

"I hate ambushes," Max said. "Know who's great at spotting ambushes? The Pathfinder Corps. Paranoid bunch."

"When your job's to map out planets and you don't know what flora or fauna is poisonous, predatory, or altogether grumpy, I imagine you develop a healthy sense of skepticism," Duke said.

"Why would you say that?" Garrison complained to Max. "Don't say the A-word. Just don't."

"It's a good place for an ambush," King said without stopping. "We need to get through it quickly."

Darkness fell hard and fast in the mountains. Hoffman and the others adjusted their optics and maintained radio silence. The area was dangerous, but the Sanheel preferred to charge like massed cavalry, which they couldn't do as well in the mountains. Hoffman reasoned there could be Rakka—the brutish, barely intelligent foot soldiers in the Kesaht force—but those troops weren't much for subtlety. He'd likely hear them massing for an attack.

Narrow trees swayed and underbrush quivered in the wind gusting through the valley, confounding Hoffman's enhanced optics nearly as much as it would natural vision. For an empty forest, the slopes seemed alive with movement.

"Hold," King said.

"Do you need me up there?" Hoffman asked.

"No. I'm sending an image to everyone in the team."

Hoffman studied the steep path cutting between two large rocks. A small force could defend the spot against most types of enemies. "How far up does this go?"

"Quite a ways. We can backtrack and go around, but it'll take hours."

"Garrison, move up to support King," Hoffman said. "Mark rally points if we have to advance rapidly back the way we came."

"Yes, sir."

Hoffman glanced at the HUD icons of his team members. "Team, move."

King rushed upward, legs pumping for speed. Garrison followed close behind but slightly to one side of the trail. Hoffman lost sight of them each time the rock-walled channel twisted.

"This next part is straight and really steep," King panted.

Hoffman rounded the corner in time to see Garrison seize the drag-strap on the back of King's gear and pull him down before a massive boulder rolled over them. The pair of Strike Marines smashed themselves into an eroded depression on the floor of the micro canyon.

"Back ten meters and tuck into the wall!" the lieutenant ordered.

"Tucking in!" Booker and the others shouted on top of each other.

The boulder rumbled past his position, scraping the front of his helmet as he pressed himself into a groove. As soon as it was gone, he sprinted to King and Garrison. "Sound off!"

"King."

"Garrison."

A moment passed.

"Booker."

"Duke."

"Max."

"Opal—sir okay?"

"Sir is OK. Where's Gor'al? Can someone see him?"

"Opal see Gor. Opal bring back Gor."

"I have visual," Booker said. "Opie's climbing down to check on him."

"Is he moving?" Hoffman asked.

Booker was laughing with relief when she answered. "He's all ass-backward and shaking his head. I think he might have gone eight-ball-to-the-corner-pocket. I'm on my way to check him."

"I'm taking Garrison to the top of this draw before we repeat being on the wrong end of the bowling alley,"

King said.

"There won't be another boulder," Duke said.

"How can you know that?" Max argued in his high-pitched voice.

"I've been counting boulders. The likelihood they found two that will roll down this pass is slim. Definitely worth risking a comms guy and a doughboy," Duke said.

"Almost at the top," Garrison grunted.

"We're coming." Hoffman sprinted up the trail, hours of running off his frustrations on the *Breitenfeld* and other ships paying off. He caught Garrison and King, passing them easily.

"Slow down there…boss," Garrison said.

"Go with him," King said.

"Running's not my thing."

"It is today. Stop being a meathead and go. I'm right behind you," King ordered.

Hoffman reached the top and saw where the boulder

had been pried loose. Garrison arrived gasping for breath a moment later.

"Cover me," said Hoffman. "I want to clear out that corner. Looks shady."

Garrison laughed. "You're killing me, LT! Boss has jokes."

Hoffman sidestepped as he approached hanging rocks. It looked like the type of juncture that might have a rope bridge higher up.

He paused at the edge of the shadowy space but not in time to arrest his forward momentum. Swearing, he slid feet first, using one hand to grab the wall and the other to aim his gun into the blackness.

"LT!"

Hoffman bumped several obstructions as he slid, but his armor held. It was dark, even with night vision, and objects jabbed against his armor and stuck to him. Activating his helmet lights—something he rarely did during combat—he saw he was covered in splintered wood and sticky goo.

King arrived at the top of the hole. "What the hell did you do to the lieutenant? Why is our team leader in a pit full of punji sticks? Why are you not dragging said team leader out of…that?"

"Laugh it up, gentlemen. I'm sure there's a punji pit on this planet for each of you." Hoffman pulled slime from his weapon, then his visor, and finally his armor. "Does anyone have a wet wipe?"

By the time Hoffman climbed out, every member of the team except Opal and Gor'al had become entangled in a version of the trap.

"It just fell on me! I'm not in the mood, Garrison," Booker spat. "I can't have this crap on my med kit. I didn't fall in a hole like Hoff and Duke."

"I can't have it on my comms," Max complained.

Hoffman searched for and found Duke. "You fell in

too?"

"Not. Talking. About it—behind you!"

"What?" Hoffman asked just before he spun around, throwing up his right arm as he raised his gauss rifle with his left. A second before he got both hands on the weapon, he was forced to block…

…a stone axe.

The axe haft struck his forearm and the sharpened stone stopped an inch from his visor. A gray-green hand with four fingers gripped the weapon. A lithe Karigole—its skin covered in scales, a hint of reptile in its humanoid face—stared at Hoffman with wide black eyes.

A war cry echoed off the mountain and more Karigole sprang over the rocks, all armed with simple weapons.

Hoffman shoved the warrior away, using just enough strength from his armor to separate himself from the threat. The Karigole flashed pointed teeth at Hoffman, hissed, and then reached back with the axe and hurled it at the Strike Marine.

Hoffman swiped his hand across his chest and smashed the axe into pieces. The Karigole froze and his face fell. Hoffman wasn't an expert on the alien's body language, but he was sure the Karigole just realized it had made a huge mistake.

"Stop!" Hoffman shouted. "We're Strike Marines and we—"

Something whacked into the side of his helmet and sent him stumbling. He saw the Karigole rushing toward him, an obsidian knife in one hand. The Karigole lunged forward, blade aimed at the seams of Hoffman's neck armor.

A massive hand caught the Karigole by the wrist and hoisted the alien up into the air. Opal held the alien up like a fish caught on a line.

"Karigole bad?" Opal asked as the alien hissed and

thrashed around like a cat held by the tail.

"No, no, Opal, don't hurt him." Hoffman touched the side of his helmet and felt an arrow embedded in his IR transceiver. "Hold fire! Everyone, hold your—"

"Stop!" A new voice thundered through the canyon. "*Thrag maka tan shi!*"

Hoffman turned around as a figure in old-style Strike Marine armor emerged, a beat-up gauss rifle in his hands.

The Karigole warriors slunk back from the new arrival, eyes averting him.

"Trag maka tan shi." The Strike Marine pointed at Opal. "Drop that one, war beast."

Opal looked to Hoffman.

"Let him go, Opal."

The doughboy tossed the Karigole against a boulder. The alien clutched his wrist to his chest and worked his hand open and shut.

The Strike Marine in the old armor came up to the Karigole that assaulted Hoffman and turned his chin upwards. A Ka-Bar blade snapped out of a forearm housing, stopping perilously close to the alien's bare neck.

"Whoa, wait a second," Hoffman said, raising a hand.

"This one is rude," the Strike Marine said with a heavy accent. "Impetuous and stupid. My son is too much like me." The blade retracted and the Strike Marine slapped the Karigole on the back of his head. The Strike Marine held up a hand and made three quick gestures. The aliens vanished into the mountains without a sound.

The Strike Marine lifted his other hand, a bionic replacement with five fingers instead of four, and removed his helmet, revealing a much older Karigole with an augmentic right eye.

"Steuben, I presume," Hoffman said. He removed his own helmet, frowning at the wooden arrow embedded in it.

The Karigole looked Hoffman up and down. "Who are you? No one asked you to come here."

"Not the welcome we'd expected." Hoffman pulled the arrow free and tossed it to one side. "We saw the dead Sanheel in your village. Maybe you all could use the help?"

"Sanheel, that is their name?" Steuben asked. "They attacked without warning several days ago. Captured one of my people before they got away. I've not been allowed to lead a hunt and take their skins."

"I don't know how the Kesaht or the Sanheel even knew about you all here," Hoffman said. "We've been fighting them across Union space for months now."

"So you brought this fight to us?" Steuben asked. "We smashed our radios to sever all contact with the outside galaxy. And still the war found us. Just as I warned the *gethaar*."

"Do we even look like those ponies?" Garrison

asked. "And what is this slime and how do we get the smell out of our armor?"

"The youths of my tribe have never seen Strike Marines in your new armor." Steuben touched his older model gear. "We live simply. They did not recognize the design. They attacked before I could stop them. Are any of you hurt?"

"Good to go." Booker gave Hoffman a thumbs-up.

"Then why are you complaining?" Steuben asked.

"Let me cut to the chase." Hoffman lifted his rifle barrel to the sky. "We need you—Steuben—to come with us to—"

"Useless." Steuben hit Hoffman in the chest with the palm of his hand just enough to upset the lieutenant's balance. "Do not speak to me."

"We can deal with the Kesaht first," Hoffman said. "But the Terran Union has a situation that needs your unique skill set."

"Again, do not speak to me of this," Steuben said. "I cannot agree to anything. If you make the offer to me, it is an insult to the *gethaar*."

"The…who?" Hoffman asked.

"The Karigole owe a debt to the Union. To Strike Marines. I thought there were only two of us left in all of existence before Valdar and the *Breitenfeld* led Lafayette and I to more. You make your request to the *gethaar*, Hoffman. That is all I can do for you," Steuben said.

Hoffman maintained a poker face. His pre-mission briefings hadn't mentioned these *gethaar*. The plan hadn't factored in Kesaht either.

"Just another day in the Corps," Hoffman said.

"Come. I must prepare you for the council," Steuben said. "Are you wearing any clothes beneath your armor?"

****

Hoffman and his team followed Steuben into a ravine. Karigole watched them from above, spears and nocked bows in hand.

"Man, he's from the Ember War," Garrison whispered into his mic. "Like, he was there at the end on the Xaros world ship. You ever see those stained-glass portraits in the chapels where an armor's killing one of the Xaros big-bads? I swear Steuben's in the background. Max, get his autograph for your kids."

"I am on your team IR network," Steuben said.

"Yeah, right. Sorry. Can you…"

"No."

"Just one?" Garrison pleaded. "My…friend would really appreciate it. No, for the children. That's the ticket. It's for the kids."

"The only time Karigole write their name is when they carve it into the flesh of defeated enemy to mark a victory. Still want one?"

Max made a swallowing sound. "Maybe just a selfie? What do you say, Garrison? Time to shut the hell up now?"

"That's exactly what time it is," King interjected. "When we get back to the ship, I am going to PT you to death. Twice."

"I like this one," Steuben said. "Reminds me of another sergeant you might have heard of."

The trail wound downward into the ravine then twisted upward into a secluded section. A final stretch of rough, semi-natural steps led to a broad cave entrance. Sanheel heads decorated pikes on both sides of the approach.

"We ambushed a small group to the east. Some escaped," Steuben said, barely looking at the macabre spectacle. His demeanor was disrespectful and nonchalant. "Stop here. I must explain the rules."

Hoffman signaled his team to stop.

"Only the lieutenant will come with me. The rest of you are to remain here. Do not speak to my people. Do not make eye contact with them. They may shoot an arrow or throw a spear at your feet to test your restraint. Just ignore them."

"They're just counting coup." Gor'al wagged a finger in the air. "Like the plains Indians of—"

King put a heavy hand on top of the Dotari's helmet.

"Your technology is forbidden beyond this point." Steuben gestured to Hoffman's armor. "Remove it. All of it."

"If the Kesaht show up and I'm in my pajamas," Hoffman said, "I won't be much help in that fight."

"We are watching." Steuben's organic eye darted to the Karigole staring at them. "The Strike Marine standard is to don power armor in less than one hundred and eighty seconds. Have standards slipped?"

"They have not." Hoffman stuck fingers beneath his breastplate and pulled a cord. Plates of power armor fell off and landed in the dirt, leaving him in the pseudo-muscle layer, boots, and helmet. He organized his armor into the shape of a prostrate man and set his helmet down to make the head. After removing his boots, he looked at Steuben, who held out a leather loincloth.

"You're kidding." Hoffman eyed the rough-looking garment.

"This is not Earth humor." Steuben pulled the emergency release on his own armor and tossed the loincloth to Hoffman. The Karigole removed his bionic eye and dropped it into his helmet, then snapped off his mechanical hand and tossed it onto the pile. He stripped off his pseudo-muscle layer and walked stark naked into the cave. Someone tossed him a set of leather breeches as he vanished into the darkness.

"That's going to stay with me," Duke said. "And not in a good way."

"Don't worry, sir," Booker said, turning around. "I won't peek."

"Just another day in the Corps," Hoffman said through gritted teeth and stripped down.

He adjusted the loincloth and followed Steuben inside. A group of Karigole females, with short white hair and wraps crisscrossed over their chests, examined Steuben where he stood just inside the cave.

"There," Steuben said, pointing to a ring of flowers on the floor. "They will look you over."

"What's all this about?" Hoffman said as he entered the ring. A pair of Karigole touched his arms with sticks and prodded him to raise them up to his sides. One of the females leaned close to the side of his neck and sniffed. She spoke to Steuben quickly.

"Your face is wrong," Steuben said. "Why?"

"Why what?"

"The *gethaar* are with child. They will not allow deformity into their presence. They believe it can harm the baby. Answer me or these handmaids will reject you. You want another of your Marines to take your place?"

"Yeah, I'll send Garrison in here. That'll work great. I was a doughboy officer during the Ember War. My face and voice were changed to match that of Jared Hale. After the war, I got my looks back," Hoffman said.

"Jared Hale…I remember him." Steuben bent forward and a handmaid looked into his empty eye socket as the Karigole sibilant language continued around Hoffman. He felt a stick touch his lower back.

"What happened there?" Steuben asked.

"Stabbed by a Naroosha spike drone." The stick traced down the back of his right arm. "Vishrakath claw." The touch went away.

"They say you are very ugly." Steuben switched to

his native language for a moment. "But you do not appear to be genetically inferior."

"I'll take that as a compliment."

"You are very lean. You must work out," Steuben said. "What? Is this not proper to say? Many Marines have told me to say such things to disrobed human men."

"I'll explain the faux pas later. Can we see the *gethaar* now?" Hoffman asked.

"You may pass. Now you need to relax," Steuben said.

"Relax? It's bad enough I'm dressed like someone's about to stick bills in my thong and now—" A hood came down over his head and rough hands lifted him off the ground.

"Don't struggle so much. Maybe struggle a little. Make them feel like they're earning their honor today. But don't struggle too much. It will take longer," Steuben said.

****

Hoffman's wrists and ankles were bound to a rough stick and he swayed from side to side as Karigole carried him deeper into the cave. He couldn't see, but he heard aliens moving around and Steuben answering to shouts that echoed off the walls. The air was damp and growing colder, which came as a slight comfort, as the sensation of fire might mean he was the guest of honor at some sort of Karigole feast, and he'd likely be on the menu.

"Steuben?" Hoffman asked.

"They like you! You are pink, like a little baby," the Karigole answered.

Sounds were strange this deep underground. Dripping water sounded too loud while Steuben's voice sounded far away when it was right next to him.

"You are doing much better than Ken Hale would have done," Steuben said.

"You mean this never happened to him?"

"It would have if he'd been allowed to visit. The *gethaar* decided we should have no further contact with the outside galaxy once our home was established here. They ordered our radios smashed…I was opposed to that decision."

Hoffman felt his path go down several steps, then a wave of cool, fresh air passed over his body. He heard a knife whack into the pole and he fell into dirt. Someone yanked off the hood. A Karigole behind him wrapped an arm around his neck and pulled back to lift his chin. He felt the knife touching his throat.

He looked around as best he could. He was in a round space, and rock walls reached straight up to the sky. When he craned his neck up, he saw stars. They were in some sort of a small caldera within the mountain range, the top of a dead volcano. Torches provided light, sending shadows dancing over beautifully ornate paintings done with simple dyes and paint. He remembered a childhood trip to view pictographs in the Valley of Fire in Nevada, but those were long gone. Erased by the Xaros. The Karigole paintings were anything but primitive.

Steuben stood nearby, his arms crossed. He wagged a claw-tipped finger at Hoffman and the grip around his neck vanished.

"You're treated as out-clan. So this is completely normal," Steuben said.

"Oh, good. Thought I was in trouble." Hoffman looked around the room, studying details of the space in case he needed to escape. Armed Karigole stood beside a tunnel opening. Screens made up of woven grass blocked another tunnel on the other side of the caldera. Unless he was going to climb up and out of the volcano shaft, he was going to have a hard time getting out.

Adult Karigole came out from behind the screens—more handmaidens and armed males—all armed with spears and knives.

"Say nothing. Pretend you're invisible," Steuben said.

A Karigole holding a spear decorated with bright-colored feathers banged the haft against the rock floor twice, and Steuben went to his knees then pressed his forehead to the ground.

Three aliens came out from behind the screens, all shorter than the other Karigole and with wide hips, full breasts, and pregnant bellies. Each carried a baby on one hip, and toddlers followed them, clutching to hands and woven skirts.

The *gethaar*.

The young Karigole stared at Hoffman with wide eyes, some ducking behind the *gethaar* and peeking out at him.

The three *gethaar* handed the children off, then sat down in a semicircle in front of Hoffman. Adult males sat behind them and used their backs to prop up the pregnant matriarchs. The one in the middle clicked her claws twice and Steuben ended his kowtow.

"You have brought death to us," the middle *gethaar* said.

"I don't…" Hoffman looked at Steuben but couldn't read the alien's expression. "My name is Lieutenant Thomas Hoffman. Terran Strike Marines. *We* come in peace." He paused and studied his audience. No reaction. "We didn't know the Kesaht were here. They arrived before us. How—"

The *gethaar* to the left hissed at him through sharp teeth. "You know the thieves' name. Your Terra is at war with them, yes?"

"They attacked us. Unprovoked. We've beaten them on many worlds, but the war continues."

"The Kesaht spilled our blood because your metal guards our skies," a *gethaar* said. "Why did your metal fail? The last hairless ape that was here promised we would be safe."

"I don't know," Hoffman said. "Let me go find the Kesaht. I'll ask them."

"Good spirit," a *gethaar* said. Her belly bulged slightly as the baby within pushed against the inside of her womb. She put her palm against the unborn's touch.

"You waste words. You did not come here for the Kesaht," said the middle—and oldest-looking—one. "What do you want from us?"

"The Terran Union needs Steuben's help. One of our worlds is under threat from some sort of a beast and—"

The women chattered, hissed, and made hand gestures that were suspiciously like something his Strike Marines might do. One of the women repeatedly drew her flat hand across her throat—which he wanted to interpret as "be quiet" instead of "kill him."

"We need his skill as a hunter to—"

"No. The one you call Steuben is our head man. He trains our children to fight. To be Karigole. He is the last of his cohort and the only warrior that can fight with your metal."

"He will be safe and he will return." Hoffman looked to Steuben, then back to the matriarchs. "The situation on planet Eridu can change the entire balance of the war against the Kesaht." Hoffman looked at each of the *gethaar*, seeing no indication that he was successfully making his case.

"There is a debt," Hoffman said. "A blood debt. Steuben was part of a mission. A Strike Marine named Rohen died to—"

"Stop," Steuben snapped. "You will not speak of that place in front of the *gethaar*. Ever. One more word and your tongue will be mine."

"We know what you've done for us," a *gethaar* said. "One of you called Val-dar. His bright-en-feld took us from hell. We cannot release Steuben. Not after our loss. The Kesaht stole a child from us, a *gethaar* child. Do you know us well? Our babies are not born male or female. They develop their gender later in life. But a *gethaar* is always born a *gethaar*. We are the only Karigole that gives birth. She was the first born since the Reaping…and now she is gone."

"Then she's…alive," Hoffman said. "The Kesaht don't kill children. They take them alive back to their home world. We still don't know why. But if the Kesaht are still on this planet, I will find them. Bring her back to you."

"What is your price?" the lead matriarch asked.

"I kill Kesaht for free," Hoffman said. "Children are not bargaining chips."

The *gethaar* leaned close to each other and spoke in their own language. Hoffman looked at Steuben and raised an eyebrow.

"They say…" Steuben cocked his head slightly.

"They say I may have been right about humans. Remarkable."

"How so?"

"You must not be married. For a woman to admit a man is right about anything…"

The *gethaar* broke out of their huddle and raised their hands to the sky.

"*Un'a'shanala!*" they cried in unison.

The rest of the Karigole thrust weapons high and repeated the call.

"Is that good?" Hoffman asked.

"Dinnertime." Steuben stood and went behind Hoffman. He set one hand on the Marine's bare shoulder. "Is human meat salty?"

"What?" Hoffman tried to get up, but Steuben kept him pinned to the ground.

A *gethaar* was helped to her feet, then she waddled over to Hoffman. The matriarch dipped a claw into a small leather pouch; it emerged with a fine yellow powder clinging to it. She scratched down either side of Hoffman's nose then across his forehead.

"That's not seasoning," Steuben said. "You've been given permission to hunt in our lands."

"So…I'm not going to be eaten?"

"Ha. Ha. Ha. I kid. Earth humor." Steuben hooked his one hand under Hoffman's shoulder and lifted him to his feet with relative ease. "No, I will help you track down the Kesaht and rescue the child. Come, it's best to stalk prey during sunrise."

****

King tensed as the sound of an arrow whistled through the air. There was *thwap* as the projectile buried into the ground a few yards away. Dozens more arrows were in the ground, tracing a shape King couldn't quite make out.

The team stood in a loose circle around Hoffman and Steuben's power armor, backs to each other as they kept an eye on the Karigole moving around the rocks.

"I'm telling you," Max said, "they are not just messing with us. This is like some weird sort of initiation."

"And I'm telling you those crazy kids are using arrows to make a connect-the-dot drawing of a dick," Garrison said as he wagged a finger at the arrows.

"I very much doubt it is a phallus," Gor'al said.

"They are young, hotheaded fighters," Garrison said. "You ever been around junior Marines or soldiers? They draw dicks on everything."

"There were some interesting pictures in the latrines during our last field exercise," the Dotari said.

"Dicks, Gor, they were dicks," Garrison said.

"Were you the one drawing them?" King asked.

"I am a seasoned Strike Marine, Gunney," Garrison

said. "I have much more culture than that…I may have added a few Chuck Norris facts to the port-a-potties."

"Yes, the famous warrior," Gor'al said. "Is it true he beat a brick wall in a game of tennis?"

"Absolutely. Then he ate a whole cake before his friends could tell him there was a stripper in it." Garrison flinched as another arrow hit the ground.

"OK, none of us even knows what Karigole junk looks like," Booker said. "That could be some sort of a local bird or a—"

"Cocks are birds," Garrison said, shrugging.

"Where is sir?" Opal grumbled.

"Hang tight, big guy," Booker said. "He'll be back soon, you big puppy."

Gor'al lifted the visor on his helmet to rub his face, then slapped it back down.

Duke reached into a pouch on his belt, then shook his hand around inside it.

"Where's my dip?" the sniper asked, turning his head slowly toward Gor'al. The alien was still as a statue. "Where. Is. It?"

Gor'al's beak worked once.

"You son of a parakeet." Duke swiped at the Dotari, but Gor'al ducked the blow.

"It is a *gar'udda* nut," Gor'al said. "I am simply hungry. Would you like one?"

"I'd rather eat a moose nugget than your pogie bait." Duke took a step out of the circle, but a sharp look from King put him back in place. "You swiped my dip!"

"No, special spice blend from back home." Gor'al swallowed hard. "Yummy."

"Pop your visor." Duke reached to Gor'al again. "Let me smell your breath!"

"Is this making the Karigole more or less likely to eat us?" Max mused.

"I am innocent of this baseless accusation," Gor'al

said.

"Let me. Smell. Your breath, Gor." Duke pointed at the Dotari's face.

"Here comes the LT," Booker said. "Thank God. Steuben's with him."

Hoffman moved smartly out of the cave and toward his team, doing a double take at the arrows in the ground nearby.

"What did I miss?" he asked, stepping between King and Opal and picking up his pseudo-muscle layer.

"No overtly hostile act," King said.

"Some sort of pictograph." Garrison waved a hand at the arrows. "Could you tell us what it is, Mr. Steuben, sir? Out of curiosity."

Steuben snapped his prosthetic hand into the stump beneath his elbow and turned his good eye to the arrows.

"It is a rune for valor, luck on the battlefield," the Karigole said. "Why? What did you think it was?"

"Nothing!" Garrison's voice was so high-pitched it almost squeaked.

"This is going in my report back to Dotari High Command," Gor'al said. "I learned a lot about humans today."

"Have you learned not to steal dip yet?" Duke grumbled.

"Baseless accusation," Gor'al said. "It's not like I took the pouch of mint-flavored long cut from your sniper bag."

Duke's eyes went wide and he slapped the bottom of the bag slung over his shoulder.

A Karigole called out from atop a rock.

"Are you all prepared for a hike?" Steuben said. "My scouts found trace of the Sanheel."

"I thought your fighters weren't allowed far from this cave?" Hoffman said.

"I anticipated the *gethaar* would grant us a hunt."

Steuben stepped into his boots and slapped on a thigh plate. "I sent out scouts when you first arrived. Don't tell the matriarchs."

"Tell them what?" Hoffman strapped on his breastplate.

"You show promise." Steuben picked up a sheathed scimitar the length of Hoffman's arm and snapped it onto his back.

Chapter 5

The Strike Marines and their Karigole guide stopped just below a hilltop as dawn broke over the horizon, casting orange light through the receding night.

Max unfolded his gear and pulled up the holo screen. Garrison, Booker, and Opal spread out to secure the perimeter while Duke maintained overwatch of the area in general. Hoffman and the rest waited for the communications device to come to life.

"If it is an appropriate thing to say, at this moment, you look much better in your armor," Gor'al said to Hoffman. "Very manly. There was some debate as to whether you'd return all oily."

Hoffman glared at the Dotari as his Strike Marines

suddenly became interested in other parts of the clearing. Duke whistled nonchalantly.

Hoffman formed his words deliberately. "Max, how is the connection?"

It took a second for his commo guy to answer. "Pretty good, sir. I mean, whenever you're ready."

"What?"

"Nothing, sir. It's just that I've had that dream—you know the one. When you go to school or something in your underwear…"

"No worries. It's actually quite liberating. In fact, there may be some interesting training cycles in the future…the entire team in the twenty-kilometer loincloth run."

"Hoorah, sir," said Max, though his response lacked the usual gusto.

A low whistle like a bosun's call sounded from the holo projector.

"*Scipio* Actual for Hammer One," said the image of Tagawa said.

"Hammer One, go."

"You're way behind the mission clock. Advise reason."

"Complications. Will need to modify timetable."

Radiation from the atmosphere garbled what the captain said next. Hoffman put one hand to the ear area of his helmet but kept his eyes on the projection of Tagawa.

"I said we're on a time schedule. Can you expedite results?"

"Negative. Search and rescue of critical civilian personnel needed. There are horsemen on the planet," Hoffman said, using the most current designation for the Sanheel.

"That…is not what we anticipated," Tagawa said.

"I need the *Scipio* to run interdiction. If the Kesaht vessel gets off world and to the Crucible, this mission is a failure."

"Are you aware of the size and armament of the Kesaht ship? My *Scipio* isn't exactly built to take on much," Tagawa said.

"That's a negative. We'll pass on any further intelligence we find, but locals encountered upwards of twenty horsemen at one time. Whatever ship they came in can't be that big."

"Be advised I will signal Earth for reinforcements. Twenty Sanheel seems like a tall order for one team of Strike Marines."

"One team of Strike Marines *and* a Karigole warrior. Besides, it will take days to spin up a larger force and then they can't land anywhere but the one LZ without the orbitals blowing them up. We're default aggressive. Maybe we can catch them while they're napping. We flood the area with more Marines, the enemy may know we're getting close to them."

Tagawa's response was lost in static.

Max adjusted his gear, clearly nervous that the interference was indicative of a more serious Kesaht threat. The Kesaht's standard procedure was to ionize the atmosphere and eliminate communications before a major assault.

"Requesting a passive scan of the planet for critical intel needed to complete this mission," Hoffman said. "Confirm, requesting a passive scan."

Tagawa nodded. "Good call, I think. You have a better feel for the situation down there. It will take a while, but we can do it."

Steuben furrowed his distinctive brow and made one of his guttural, nonverbal thinking sounds. "Why not an active scan?"

"Could be detected. I don't want them to know we're looking for them."

Steuben nodded slowly. "You're not an idiot."

"Thanks…I think." He faced the IR holo, saluted the *Scipio*'s captain, and signed off.

"How long will this take?" Steuben asked.

"A while." Hoffman produced the blasted piece of metal his team had located earlier. "We recovered this on our way in."

Steuben took the scrap and sniffed it. "It bears the Kesaht scent." He turned it over several times.

"We searched for larger pieces to do a more complete analysis, but it was pretty scattered."

"One moment." Steuben muttered several Karigole curses as he interfaced his old armor with the newer versions Hoffman's team wore. "There it is. I am sending video."

Hoffman watch the camera feed without comment. A Kesaht ship, smaller than the *Scipio*, raced upward from the planet's surface and attempted to skirt a storm. Lightning reached out and grabbed it. By the end of the flash, the ship had disappeared into the clouds.

"Roll it again," Hoffman said. Steuben complied. "There. Looks like its trailing fire. The ship was definitely hit."

"You have good eyes for a human."

"They were damaged." Hoffman pulled up a map of the planet. "Where could they set down? Does it match with your scout reports?"

Steuben leaned closer, uncrossing his arms. "If they couldn't make orbit, they could be anywhere on the planet. But the direction of travel from the video matches my scouts' report."

"Best not to run around like chickens with our heads cut off," King said. "We have an area to search."

Steuben began swiping at the map Hoffman had pulled up. "There has been no sign of Sanheel since the ship took off."

"All dead or they got what they came for," King

said. "They took a child?"

"Not just any child, a *gethaar*, the rarest and most precious of the Karigole. One may be born two or three times to a mother *gethaar* in the hundreds of times she will be pregnant. Why do you look at me like that?"

"Hundreds?" Booker asked, her face screwed up in shock.

"We are long-lived. I am nearly nine hundred Earth years old," Steuben said.

"What is it with the Kesaht always taking kids?" Max asked. "I heard about them doing that on Oricon."

Steuben shifted his weight, clenching and unclenching his fists in frustration. "Why would they do this? Tell me of the Kesaht."

"They attacked without warning," Hoffman said. "We'd never encountered them before they went hostile. They're unknown to the Bastion Alliance as well. There isn't much more that's official, but there was this…spy. A traitor told me there's someone driving the Kesaht against us. I don't know if I should even share it. Spies aren't to be trusted."

"Tell me," Steuben said.

"Keep in mind she could've been blowing smoke," Hoffman said, "but Masha was positive there was a Toth overlord—"

Steuben's lips retracted, revealing rows of pointed teeth. "A Toth?" he snarled. "No. I saw the last of them die. All of them."

"Huh, she said they were nearly extinct." Hoffman frowned. "Wait, then do you know about some sort of entity that—"

"Malal." Steuben got to his feet and slashed his claw tips in front of his real eye. "Do not speak of that monster…if the Toth live, then this changes things. It changes everything."

Hoffman looked at King. They shrugged at each

other.

"Does it change how we're going to find the baby *gethaar*?" Hoffman asked.

"No." Steuben drew his scimitar and spat on the blade, revealing intricate writing etched into the metal. "But I need at least one Sanheel alive to rip out information. If the Kesaht serve the Toth, then they must die. All of them."

"I like where he's going with this," Duke said.

Steuben wiped the spittle across the etchings, then returned the blade to its scabbard.

"A Toth overlord survived." He shook his head. "I was too quick to believe the vendetta over. I should never have given up the hunt, but the *gethaar* and my people needed me. Lafayette curses me from the afterlife…We must move," the Karigole said, "before the light changes too much."

Chapter 6

Hoffman scanned the cloud-filled sky as morning's light cast an orange hue through the overcast.

"Stand by for drop," King announced. "Duke, do you have visual?"

"Of course I have visual. Snipers see all."

"I thought a sniper was a snake," Booker said. "And I thought snakes didn't look at the sky."

"I take you on one mission and mentor you and this is what I get," Duke said. "You're turning my actions against me. The sniper is a snake, a sky-watching snake who sees one supply module inbound. Sending coordinates now."

A waypoint pinged on Hoffman's visor.

"Tagawa's right," the lieutenant said. "A logistics drop is too small for the orbitals to register as a threat."

"Hooray for small favors," Max said. "Let's hope we didn't use up our luck for the entire day."

"It's off-target by half a kilometer. We need to move and set up around the landing zone," King said. "LT, I guess that means you since you're the fastest."

"Booker and Opal can keep up," Hoffman said as the entire team started moving.

"That thing can run?" Steuben asked, pointing at Opal.

"He doesn't know when to quit. Pain's little more than an abstract idea for doughboys, disregarded when not useful," Hoffman said. There were times he didn't believe this, but that was what he'd been taught during his initial training phase. Many of his peers used it to console themselves when the doughboys suffered worse than other soldiers.

It felt good to run. He stretched out in the lead and soon saw the vapor trail of the rapidly descending supply pod.

"We're almost at the LZ." He surveyed the area, looking for anything that would ruin the resupply. It was a good location. "We're set. What's your ETA, Hammer Two?"

"Momentarily."

Hoffman laughed involuntarily. A mechanical spike the size of Booker slammed into the ground dead center of the perimeter they had set out. The thing had minimal antigravity plating to slow the final descent.

The rest of the team arrived. Without hesitation, Steuben opened the pod and removed the drone. With several fluid movements that belied his mechanical hand, he put a device from his armor into the drone and tossed it into the air.

Seconds later, the drone disappeared in a cloaking field.

"Oh, that's why it's called a 'Karigole cloak,'" Garrison said. "Thought they were useless for most tactical situations."

"Really, doofus?" Max said, dipping his head toward the breacher. "In front of the Karigole?"

"If the enemy is scanning for the cloaks, they are easily defeated," Steuben said, unfazed by the cross talk. "That these Kesaht serve the Toth makes a number of things clear. The Toth have used Karigole cloaks in the past. Their ship must have arrived from a wormhole in the outer solar system where it wasn't detected by the system's defenses, then flew here while cloaked. They thought they could sneak off world and through the Crucible undetected. Clever, but they've given us a scent to follow. All cloaks have a resonance frequency. The field I just loaded onto that drone can detect another cloak from line of sight over several miles. Now we wait."

"That's exactly what I was going to say," Garrison said. "Had all that worked out myself. Really."

A breeze cut across the clearing, feeling like it had swept in from the distant savanna. As everyone looked at each other, Hoffman resisted the urge to fidget or review the data for the tenth time.

Max cleared his throat. "So you were in that movie, *Last Stand on Takeni*? You seemed a lot…shorter in that."

Steuben growled but not unpleasantly—or maybe it was angrily. Hoffman was still trying to parse the Karigole body language.

"A travesty," Steuben said. "An insult. Standish should have destroyed that abomination of art when he bought the rights. Instead, he put himself into the movie."

"That guy cannot act," Duke said. "At all."

Steuben glanced at his forearm screen. "I have a

location."

Hoffman reviewed the information when it came to his screen, quickly confirming that everyone received Steuben's transmission. The old armor seemed to be integrated with the new.

He looked to the mountains and imagined the valley beyond it as was indicated by the coordinates. Magnifying his visor optics, he detected a line of wrecked trees from a crash but no ship.

"It is still cloaked," Steuben said.

"Team, let's go," Hoffman said. "Time to earn our paychecks."

Chapter 7

Steuben kept to himself during the trek across the valley. Hoffman watched him carefully, noting how easily he fit into their formation and how refined his movement was. Small things—from how he walked to how he scanned his assigned zone without rushing to failure—impressed Hoffman, and he wondered how his team would compare to other heroes of the Ember War. It was a sobering thought.

The closer they moved toward the destination, the slower he drove the team. King and Booker took point while Duke constantly searched for good overwatch locations.

The sky turned purple as they stopped to spy on their target.

"I have the eye and excellent concealment," Duke announced. "You're welcome."

"Hold and report. I want to stay updated. Keep an eye out for Sanheel on the perimeter."

"Nothing seen yet. I'll let you know."

Steuben put his frightening clawed hands on Hoffman's shoulder. "The child is essential to the Karigole's future. Her life is worth more than mine."

Hoffman nodded.

Duke reported a patrol of Sanheel. Moments later, Garrison reported a second.

"I suspect they have their zone quartered," King said. "Let's assume two more patrols, any of which might function as a QRF for the others."

Duke's gravelly voice droned out a description of the tactical environment outside the ship. "Can confirm a third and fourth element. All operating in pairs. Looks like Gunney's assessment of their QRF plan is accurate. I don't see a larger response force."

Hoffman consulted his tactical display. "Duke, remember when you told me you could make that two-thousand-meter shot?"

"Like it was yesterday."

"You have the pair of Sanheel in sector four. When they reach the edge of their zone where you can see them, take both of them. That will be the signal for other teams," Hoffman said.

"Give Booker the other long-range shot," Duke said.

"Booker, you copy?"

"Copy. I can make the shot with my gauss rifle easy. No cheating, like with Duke's toothpick," Booker said.

"Did you just insult Ice Claw?"

"King," Hoffman said, "you have sector one and Garrison has sector three. Opal, you're cleanup for sector four. Gor'al, same thing for sector two. I'll cover down on Steuben." The Sanheel patrol in sector four would be entering Duke's kill zone in seconds.

"Stand by. Taking the shot in three, two, one…"

Duke's sniper rifle cracked twice and the rest of the team fired almost simultaneously. Hoffman scanned the area for a reaction from the Sanheel and counted to ten.

"Good work, team. Let's move in slow. Hate to waste all that marksmanship because someone stepped on a twig," Hoffman said.

Steuben moved beside him as they crept through the darkening night. "You are a decent Strike Marine. I think I can work with you."

"Thanks. You're the best one-handed Karigole I've been in the field with."

"How many have you worked with?"

"Counting you? One."

"Earth humor. I am laughing on the inside."

Hoffman chuckled. "You're all right, Steuben."

"Your team must orient themselves before we continue. The displacement field is hard on the senses," Steuben said.

"Team, hold your positions." Hoffman reviewed video feeds from each of their helmets. Looking at the ship made him dizzy.

"Garrison, don't look away from that breach."

The camera view swept across the damaged ship, eventually focusing on an intact piece of the fuselage.

"Garrison," Hoffman said sternly.

Slowly, the camera feed moved left and resolved on a hole ripped in the side of the Kesaht ship.

"I know you want to blow everything up, but remember when we ran out of denethrite on *Kid'ran's Gift*? How much fun was that?" Hoffman asked.

"You're right, LT. I think this opening could be improved. It's a little small for Opal and Steuben," Garrison said.

Steuben shifted restlessly. "Too much caution. The *gethaar* is in danger. Tell me your plan now or I will make my own."

"The Sanheel normally use Rakka on their outer perimeter. They're also fond of charging and always have a troop of them ready to go. Their lack of Rakka or QRF suggests limited manpower," Hoffman said.

"What is a Rakka?" Steuben asked.

"An ugly, bipedal humanoid that likes to fight…and wear body parts as trophies."

"There is something wrong with that?" Steuben asked. "I joke. Very funny, you think."

"Hilarious. I'm sending in two Marines on a stealth mission to see what we have. If this is a hostage rescue, it'd help to know where the hostage is and how fast we need to reach her before the Ixio that's normally in charge of a ship this size decides to hurt the hostage," Hoffman said.

"What is an Ixio?" Steuben said. "Are you making these names up?"

"Garrison and Booker, you're up."

"You send the guy who explodes things?" Steuben asks.

"I have my reasons."

"I'd sure like to know what they are," Booker said. "Kidding. We've trained for this, Steuben. I'm small and Garrison is good at getting into places with or without explosives."

"I've got tools and skills for breaching doors—and natural good looks for those high-class party infiltrations."

Max snorted. "High class? That was a strip club."

"Which I had to watch from the outside despite my obvious qualifications as an inside agent."

"Very good," King interrupted, his tone silencing

the loose talk. "You're all very special. I will write a nice letter to your mothers telling them what an asset you are to the Terran Union. Now shut your mouths and execute the lieutenant's plan."

"On you, Booker," Garrison said.

The medic crept along the hull of the shimmering ship with Garrison right behind her. They looked like kids playing make-believe in the moonlight. On casual inspection, the clearing seemed empty. Only a washed-out wrongness, a wavering in the air like over an open fire, gave away the presence of the Kesaht ship.

The stealth team paused. Garrison tapped Booker on the shoulder and she ducked through the hole with him, following so closely they were almost wearing the same armor.

"We're in," Booker said. "Pretty standard Kesaht ship, maybe a light corvette class. Leaving coms and video open so you can follow along."

"There's a slight lag with the video," Hoffman said.

"Copy that," Booker said.

Hoffman expanded her image feed as large as it would go in his HUD, covering the view from other team members. She worked her way through a hallway with several doors.

"Clear up to the first intersection. The opening was in the middle of their barracks. Rakka body parts everywhere. Looks like they lost a bunch of the poor bastards to the lightning strike," she said. "Need a couple more to clear rooms."

"Hammer One, copy that. Bringing the team. Duke, maintain overwatch."

"It's what I do," he said grimly.

"Poor snipers, never invited to the real party," Booker said.

"You didn't complain on Koensuu. There was that steam room…" Duke drawled.

"Look at that—I think I found a barricaded door. Could this be our bad guy's lair?" Booker said, speaking rapidly.

Hoffman and the others gathered at the opening, stacking up like it was a fresh assault. King brought up the tail-gunner-charlie position, tapping Max in front of him, who tapped Opal and so on. When Hoffman felt Steuben's mechanical touch, he went in, concentrating on smooth, efficient movements. Before long, he found Booker and Garrison holding a long hallway.

"Let's clear these side rooms and hold on the barricaded door. They've probably seen us on their surveillance cameras," Hoffman said.

"If they're working," Garrison said.

"Let's assume they are."

Garrison pointed at a small, crude camera that had been turned to show a close-up view of the wall it was mounted on. "That one isn't. Maybe they noticed when I turned it, maybe they didn't. I know they're Kesaht, but there's still a chance they're watching bootleg copies of the *Last Stand on Takeni* instead of doing their job."

Steuben looked at Hoffman. "He's the dumb one, isn't he?"

"I'm funny and irreverent. Opal's the dumb one."

"Opal eat soon," Opal said.

"It's complicated," Hoffman said. "Let's run these rooms and meet out here. Two guns to a room unless you need more."

He took the first doorway in the same manner he had entered the ship. Steuben followed.

Triple-stacked bunk beds lined three of the walls. Beyond the cubicle was a second room that looked like a combination kitchen, shower, and toilet. "Clear, nothing seen."

Steuben led the way back to the hallway. They skipped the next cell because Gor'al and Max were already clearing it. Soon, the hallway had been swept of possible threats.

The barricaded door was at the end of a T intersection, the arms of which they hadn't cleared because those hallways probably continued around the rest of the ship's circumference.

"Opal and Gor, protect Garrison while he gets that door open. Watch the long angles."

"Guard hallway," the doughboy said.

"Yes, I will do this for you, Lieutenant Hoffman," Gor'al said.

"This will take him a long time and it is probably a safe room for their cowardly officers," Steuben said. "We should search the rest of the ship while we wait."

Hoffman thought about it. "We'll have to split up."

Steuben nodded. "Agreed. This is best."

"King, stay here with the team. Keep overwatch on Garrison. Opal, come with us."

"Yes, sir."

"I'll lead," Steuben said. "I've had some experience with alien vessels."

Hoffman cocked his head sideways in acknowledgment. He had experienced more than his own share of alien strangeness, but it was probably nothing compared to the exploits of someone like Steuben. The Karigole didn't seem like the type of warrior to sit down and tell stories over a beer. Maybe they would talk when this was over. He'd like to pick the brain of a real hero of the Ember War.

Steuben moved swiftly but didn't rush. Whenever they came to a doorway, he went inside, Hoffman following right behind him and Opal guarding the hallway. On one occasion, Hoffman called Opal inside to help with a larger room.

One area after another proved empty.

They emerged into the main hallway that followed

the contour of the ship.

"I think most of their assets are guarding the ship or are behind the barricaded door," Hoffman said.

"Garrison for Hoffman." A voice came over the IR comm.

"Go for Hoffman."

"This isn't going to be one of those 'armory' situations again, is it?" Garrison asked. "Because that was a bit of a shit show."

"It was an honest mistake," Gor'al said. "We all survived the Kesaht Armor. Ha ha. Let us remember it fondly."

"If it is, then it's the room you found. You'll have to clean it," Hoffman said.

"Booker helped find it," Garrison said.

"Do you need something or are you just wasting radio traffic?" Hoffman asked.

"I'm running a snake camera into a vent. Thought

you should know. Might piss them off and set off a massive security event."

"Thanks for the heads-up. Be careful."

****

"We're wasting time," Steuben said.

Hoffman agreed but didn't have a better option. He picked up the pace, cruising down the ship hallway, hunting through his gunsights until he found what he was hoping would be there—a mirror image of the T intersection his team was trying to penetrate.

"The Kesaht ships look random and strange, but they're pretty basic," Hoffman said. "This should be a duplicate of the first section."

"Yes. I was thinking the same." Steuben's gravelly voice betrayed the same impatience and growing dread Hoffman felt.

"As a bonus, this door isn't barricaded."

Steuben studied the area, then turned the camera toward the wall as Garrison had on the other side.

"Opal, hold this intersection."

"Yes, sir." The doughboy swept his eyes each direction and then at Hoffman, then repeated the process with his complete attention.

"It is a good sentry," Steuben said, grudgingly impressed.

"Let's see if we can get in," Hoffman said.

The door was stout enough to withstand decompression if ship integrity was lost during a void battle, and the keypad was covered with simple shapes. Hoffman applied the standard decryption software issued to all Strike Marines and it opened. "I think this is an older ship."

"Or your equipment has improved a great deal since I served with the Terran Union."

"Step back." Hoffman jammed the open button with the barrel of his gauss rifle—retreating a step as soon as the door started to slide.

"I will cut some pie," Steuben said.

"The pie. Cut *the* pie."

"I said that." With his weapon aimed but just low enough to avoid obstructing his view, Steuben took longer and longer peeks at sections of what was inside. When he reached the other side of the door, he nodded at Hoffman. "We should crisscross, I think you Marines say."

Hoffman bent his knees slightly and then nodded. Steuben went first. Hoffman crossed behind him to clear the left portion of the room. Steuben did the right side a few seconds later.

"Opal, with us."

The doughboy came quickly and covered the center. The room was full of metal cubes four feet long on a side, the corners reinforced with bronze-colored caps.

Steuben carefully approached a cube in the middle of the floor and growled. "What is this?"

"Stasis cube," Hoffman said. "Saw them on the mission debrief from when the Union fought the Kesaht on Oricon."

"She could be inside." Steuben drew his scimitar and jammed it into a seam and twisted. The cube popped open, and blue light cast across the deck. Inside was a reptile with feathers around the neck and ankles.

"Thagrich," Steuben said. "Local animal. We eat them."

"I doubt the *gethaar* is in any of these," Hoffman said. "Let's double back to the barricaded door."

Hoffman felt more anxious as they hurried back. Finding a stasis cube didn't reassure him. "These Kesaht assholes came a long way to steal kids. I can't believe that Masha…she was telling the truth. I'm not sure why that bothers me so much."

"Break spy," Opal said.

"Got to find her first, big guy," Hoffman said.

"This battle construct can harm humans?" Steuben asked. "I've encountered their shoddy programming before."

"He's conditioned to disarm and subdue a small number of specific humans," Hoffman said. "You and the rest of the Karigole are safe from him. Don't worry."

"I'm not to worry until a doughboy murders a Ruhaald notable and then half the team is in custody when we need them the most," Steuben said.

"What?" Hoffman looked from Opal to Steuben and back again.

"Never mind. Keep moving." Steuben motioned forward with his gauss rifle.

"Hammer Six for Door Team, we're almost back to you," Hoffman said into the team IR channel.

"Copy that," King answered.

By the time they arrived at the first T intersection, Hoffman was tired and discouraged. Previous experiences had conditioned him to expect bad things. He couldn't believe they hadn't been attacked a dozen times. Staying alert was wearing him out.

"Garrison, how're we doing?" he asked, leaning close to the breacher where the man squatted to examine the bottom of the doorframe.

"Good news or the bad news?" Garrison asked.

"Just tell me everything."

"Well, the bad news is I can't get in. The good news is I managed to run a snake inside and I can see who's in there and what they're doing. Wanna look?"

"Send it."

"The quality's subpar. I don't know what kind of lighting they've got, but it's creepy. Or maybe it's because I'm running the cord through a vent near the bottom of the door. Funny angle. Makes everyone look like a giant."

"It'll work," Hoffman said, watching the video and counting an alarming number of Sanheel and a few Rakka warriors. The interior was huge. That was a thing with Sanheel. They liked big spaces because they were big aliens. Toward the center of the room was a dais where an Ixio crooned to a small girl child—or what he thought was a girl child.

Steuben tensed when he saw the *gethaar*. For a moment, it seemed he'd smash the doors down and charge in guns blazing with or without the Strike Marines. Instead, the Karigole hero took a deep breath and let it out slowly, shaking with barely restrained violence.

"That's the *gethaar*?" Hoffman asked.

"It is."

"Garrison, we really need to get in there."

"I have some ideas. I could use a double-wrapped denethrite charge to push a neutral substance—one of Booker's IV bags, probably. Or I could draw a portal with det cord and set it off. Rush in there and kill everything that stands up. Just a suggestion."

"I prefer an option that didn't get the child killed," Hoffman said.

"Maybe they've got sewers we could crawl through," Booker suggested.

"I've got one better," Duke said, his comms scratchy. "A patrol is coming in. Maybe they'll open the door for you. My suggestion? Hide."

"You heard him." Hoffman pointed to the cells nearest the door. "Don't be seen. We may need to rush the door. The go word is 'Bambi.'"

"'Bambi'? Really?" Garrison said. "No offense, boss, but you should let us handle the creative stuff."

Hoffman picked a dark cell with an open door and moved deep inside, reasonably confident he wouldn't be seen unless they actively searched the area. Moments later, all was silent. His team was in place for whatever came next.

"One second," Garrison said, drawing out the word in a way that made Hoffman nervous.

"What are you doing?" Hoffman asked.

"Just leaving a little something to wedge the door. They can open it but won't be able to shut it. Once the hydraulics pull that shim inside, it's officially a doorway rather than a void-rated blast barrier."

"Hurry up."

Garrison flashed across the hallway and slid into one of the cell-like barracks. "Done!"

"Ouch!" Booker grunted. "Watch where you're going, meathead."

A pair of Sanheel stomped through the torn side of the ship, breaking loose new sections with their bulk. They grunted, sniffed the air, and scowled. Hoffman didn't like the gleam in their eyes or the way they sneered into the darkness.

Booker cursed. "You had to pick my cell."

Garrison patted her on the top of her helmet. "Couldn't see you, Doc."

"Listen," King said, "I'm aware of the excellent sound-dampening properties of a sealed helmet, but shut your mouths. Now."

The Sanheel grunted at each other for a moment, then the door opened and the patrol went inside. The door slid shut.

"Good job, Garrison," Max said. "Real nice. Where'd you go to breacher school again?"

"Patience." Garrison approached, inserted four fingers, and pulled the door back slowly.

"Why don't we wait for the patrol to get where they're going before we announce our presence," King said.

"Yes, sir. Just wanted to reassure Max. He's fragile, as we all know."

Hoffman reassessed the situation and formed a new plan. "Nice work. Steuben, Opal, and I cleared a similar set of interior rooms on the other side of the ship. They're short-staffed, so we should be able to establish a beachhead in the first set of rooms, then follow Garrison's camera snake."

"I would like the plan better if it were already done," Steuben said.

"Agreed. Garrison, how much snake did you run? Can you tell me how far inside the child is being held? One room? Two?"

Garrison looked uncomfortable. "I ran all the line I have. Lots of twists and turns in the vents. They seriously need a new HVAC guy."

"Fine. We go in and go slow until we can go fast," Hoffman said. "Best-case scenario, they never realize we're here. Grab the *gethaar* and get out. That's the best case."

"When have we ever experienced the best case?"

Booker said.

"Steam room on Koensuu," Duke said from outside.

Booker cursed. "It really annoys me that he's here but not here. I need to ball punch him."

"Easy," Garrison and Max said in harmony.

"Let's get this done," Hoffman said. "Steuben and Opal with me. We'll need to spread out but don't over extend. If anyone gets lucky and secures the *gethaar*, we exfiltrate immediately and rally on Duke's position."

****

Hoffman thought he understood what was at stake for the Karigole. He'd seen *Last Stand on Takeni* and heard stories about the four Karigole warriors who had been the last of their kind. Without the *gethaar*, their species was in jeopardy.

The floor plan was a repeat of what they had cleared

on the other side of the ship. Discarded meal trays, clothing, and equipment suggested it saw more use.

"Do not rush this," Steuben said. "We must not fail."

Hoffman signaled he understood then moved into the next room. From there, they would be able to see the main chamber. He suspected that was where Garrison's camera feed had been recording the Ixio by the stasis chamber.

"When we find them, we'll need to move quickly. We only get one chance to rescue the child," Hoffman said.

"Agreed. I want to interrogate the creature, but the *gethaar*'s survival and good health are most important," Steuben said.

Hoffman called for the rest of his team. They finished their zones quickly and assembled.

"Garrison, today's your big day."

The breacher unpacked his kit, selecting a coil of

denethrite cord and blasting strips. Booker produced two IV bags without having to be asked. By the time Hoffman was finalizing his plan in his head, Garrison had his breaching charge ready.

"I'm blowing the seams and that's all. Door should fall right out of its frame. No spall or debris to endanger the hostage. We get an opening and toss in some flash bangs and—"

"No stun grenades," Steuben said. "*Gethaar* are too fragile. It's not worth the risk."

"Better than getting everyone killed, including the child," King said. "I respect you, Steuben, but we know how to do this. The only way is to dominate with overwhelming speed, surprise, and violence of action."

Hoffman raised a hand to silence the argument. "No bang. We're going to take on some extra risk in this assault. Most of the overpressure will be on our side of the wall when it explodes. The *gethaar* should be safe."

As Garrison studied the door he was about to penetrate, he froze. His eyes traced a path to reinforced vents about seven feet off the ground. "Those are gun ports."

Hoffman looked closer and saw that several of the slots he assumed were for pressurization were reinforced and armored. Closer examination revealed blast residue around the edges.

Booker laughed nervously. "I'm glad there's no one on the other side of these. Otherwise, we'd be dead."

"Set the charge," Hoffman said then joined Steuben watching the surveillance feed. They'd located the security cameras shortly after Garrison and the others arrived and now used the Kesaht's own surveillance equipment against them. The camera view was crystal clear, though he couldn't hear what the alien was crooning to the child.

The Ixio would probably be eight feet tall if it stood straight up. It had thin limbs that reminded Hoffman of a spider's. The almond-shaped eyes appeared intelligent and sinister. The first one he'd seen up close had been a wounded pilot on Koen. The meeting hadn't gone well.

Next to the alien was the stasis chamber. The child seemed to float within the power field, its clothing and hair drifting as though in water or antigravity. Cables snaked into all sides of the box.

Hoffman flinched as the Ixio reached inside and wrapped its long fingers around the *gethaar* girl's throat.

"I will kill that abomination slowly," Steuben growled.

"Are you ready, Garrison?" Hoffman asked.

"I am, except I can't get the charge to stay attached. I need something to prop it against the wall. I can make just any hole, or I can make a hole we can all get through."

Max and Booker burst out in nervous laughter.

"Just any hole will do," Booker said, laughing even harder.

"Your team is very humorous," Steuben said. "Can we kill the Kesaht and save the *gethaar* now?"

A light blinked above one of the gun ports.

Gor'al made a clicking noise. "I think we have problems."

Each of Hoffman's Marines looked at the light, then cursed as several other port lights came on.

"We've been made!" King shouted.

Hoffman gave the go signal as thunder exploded from the gun ports. Rounds glanced off Opal's armor as he stepped in front of Hoffman.

"Protect sir! Sir, take cover!"

Seconds felt like minutes until Garrison pushed a button on his gauntlet and a section of the wall exploded inward. Confetti-like fragments sprayed inward with a section of the wall, filling the air with dust.

King and the rest of the team engaged the Sanheel defenders in a vicious firefight. The green-faced, tusked centaurs stomped the deck with alloy-shod hooves that shook the room. Surprisingly light on their feet, they danced sideways as they returned fire. King, Opal, and Max charged at them in a wedge with King taking the heaviest damage to his armor.

Steuben and Hoffman rushed toward the Ixio and the stasis chamber, stepping over Sanheel shot down in the initial moments of the assault.

Steuben growled as he closed the final distance. "Save her. Save her!"

The Ixio grabbed the *gethaar* child and held her up as a shield. Steuben slid to a stop, weapon aimed but not firing. The girl remained oddly calm.

"Negotiate," Hoffman said as he moved for a better angle. He could make a shot, but it wouldn't be an easy one. He disliked trick shooting—too much could go wrong.

Steuben moved forward, screening Hoffman with

his body. "Release her and I will grant you a quick death."

The Ixio shifted sideways in an attempt to watch both adversaries, glancing at the battle that was dangerously close to spilling into this area. "My master sent me to gather a sample from this world. This little one tells me your people were once prized possessions of the Toth. You could be again. Would you like that?"

"We were not 'possessions,'" Steuben said. "We were meat for the Toth."

The *gethaar* child raised a brow in surprise.

"Service to the Toth is better than living as savages," the Ixio said. "Let me leave with this one. I will petition Lord Bale on your behalf. No need to suffer the same fate we have planned for the human demons."

Steuben roared, spit flying from his mouth. "I will kill you along with your murdering Toth overlord! How dare you come to my home world! You will die! I will rip you apart!"

The Ixio trembled as he retreated but clutched the *gethaar* even tighter to his body.

Hoffman slipped around one shattered workstation after another, always losing the shot as the Ixio ducked and dodged around the bridge. Hoffman monitored Steuben's reaction to the words, fearing the Karigole warrior would make a mistake and act on his rage.

Just what had the Toth done to the Karigole?

The volume of Steuben's declaration decreased, but not the intensity. "I'll kill you. Rip your brain out. Smash your spleen," Steuben said. "I don't know what kind of filthy creature you are, but we will feast on your corpse!"

"Lord Bale was right about your people," the Ixio said. "I see why the stasis cubes were necessary."

Hoffman was now at a ninety-degree angle from Steuben and had line of sight on the child. The shot needed to be as perfect as it needed to be fast.

The Ixio twisted again, ruining Hoffman's shot.

"No, you bastard. Turn back," he muttered.

Hoffman waggled his barrel at Steuben, hoping the Ixio would think he was signaling the enraged Karigole.

Nothing. No response from the lithe alien as he backpedaled, exposing his legs through a rent in the deck.

Hoffman shot the Ixio in the knee and then immediately put a round in the alien's temple. Both shots happened too fast to see, calling more on instinct than skill. The luck of Saint Kallen touched him. He felt it long after he pulled the trigger.

The Ixio collapsed as deep-purple brain matter clotted against the bulkheads.

Steuben exploded forward, catching the *gethaar* with one hand before she could fall out of the dead Ixio's grasp.

Workstations exploded into sparks and flames, filling the bridge with smoke. Steuben rushed past Hoffman before he could stop the Karigole.

"Room's clear!" King shouted.

"Fall back. We have the hostage!" Out of training and instinct, Hoffman waved a hand forward through the smoke; he was certain no one could see him in the fire.

"Steuben, where are you? Steuben?"

He repeated the call over and over, but there was no answer.

Chapter 8

Hoffman adjusted his helmet filters, then rushed the hallway. Filters pumped air quickly but were inefficient due to the damage the ship had sustained from the lightning blast. In the void, this slow correction of the environment would have been fatal to everyone aboard.

He couldn't find Steuben or his team. Static crackled in his earpiece. Choosing a route through the outside corridor, he risked going it alone.

"...why is there so much smoke?" King asked someone, his voice suddenly too loud in Hoffman's ear.

"Fire retardant," Max said. *"I'm not sure it's*

calibrated to this planet's atmosphere. Death is in the details."

Hoffman didn't stop to respond. When he found his team near the rally point, Steuben had the *gethaar* child in his arms. Hoffman moved past his Marines and led them out of the ship and into the canyon. The *gethaar* stared at Opal's helmet, her eyes wide. The doughboy was taller and more massive than even Steuben.

"Keep security, there may be some stragglers," the lieutenant said. "Opal, the child is our principal. Understood?"

"Opal guard not-human child."

The team moved a few hundred yards away from the crash site as the ship went up in a column of flames and smoke, stopping behind a rock outcrop, and Steuben set the child down. She had a stoic demeanor that belied her size, which was of a human girl around eight or nine years old.

Booker knelt by the girl and held up a sensor wand.

"I need to do a quick check on you. This won't hurt. OK?"

"I am unharmed. The Ixio was under orders to deliver pristine samples to the Toth," she said.

"You speak English." Booker did a quick swipe of the wand down the child's body. "Very good English."

"The one you call Steuben taught me. Contact with the Terran Union was inevitable."

"No obvious trauma." Booker nodded to Hoffman and stepped away.

Steuben approached her, slinging his rifle as he knelt and bowed his head.

"Honored one, I failed you," Steuben said.

"What took so long?"

"You were not believed to be alive," Steuben said. "The humans told us much about your captors. That they would—"

"The Toth. Yes." The Karigole child spat on the ground. "Some live."

"How do you know this?" Steuben asked.

"The Ixio liked to talk. He spoke at length about the glorious Bale, the last Toth overlord, and how he saved the Kesaht from a civil war and united them against the threat of human monsters." She gave the Strike Marines a sidelong glance, then frowned at Gor'al.

"What did you all do?" the Dotari asked. "You're true allies to my species. Even if you don't share your chewing tobacco."

Duke slapped his sniper rifle bag and swore softly.

The child held up a finger, one not tipped with a claw like Steuben's.

"One Toth ship survived. A dreadnought full of their warriors and Bale. They are all on the Kesaht home world. I don't know where it is. The Ixio promised to take me to Bale personally."

"The Toth live…my oath remains," Steuben said. "You know what I must do."

"You have no choice." The girl shuffled her bare feet in the dirt and pouted. "I am cold, tired, and hungry. One of you. Carry me."

Max reached for the girl, but Steuben pushed him roughly aside. The Karigole picked her up and she flung her arms around his neck.

"Back to the landing pad," Steuben said. "Call down your ship."

Hoffman glanced at King, who shrugged.

****

The Strike Marines formed a loose perimeter around Steuben and the *gethaar* child at the edge of the landing pad. Duke pointed to the horizon, where a line of fire in the sky marked the *Scipio*'s approach. The *gethaar* sat on Steuben's knee, stoic, and with her head held high.

"Steuben," Gor'al said over his shoulder, "what did

the humans do to the Toth? My teammates have no idea what might have happened."

Hoffman cleared his throat loudly.

"There were no Dotari witnesses," Steuben said. "I was there on the deck of the *Breitenfeld* when the Toth received justice. When I thought they were wiped clean from the galaxy."

Hoffman stared at Gor'al and swiped his fingertips across his neck.

"The *Breitenfeld* nuked the Toth home world?" Gor'al's quills bristled.

Hoffman cleared his throat again.

"Booker, I believe the lieutenant is choking," Gor'al said.

"There was an…entity," Steuben said. "A Qa'Resh being named Malal. He was needed to destroy the Xaros drones spread throughout the galaxy."

"He missed one," Hoffman snorted.

"Malal learned to change the drone's programming from the Xaros Masters. His price was…energy. Souls. The Ibarras gave him the Toth to feast upon," Steuben said.

"Oh, them," King said. "The Ibarras are to blame for it all."

"There was no other way to beat the drones," Steuben said. "They were trillions upon trillions in the galaxy. Malal destroyed them all. I was there when he touched the Toth home world. Saw him spread across the surface and consume them all. Then we took Malal to…I don't know how to explain it. But Malal is now gone."

"Wonder why a Toth xenocide isn't common knowledge," Max said.

"Think the rest of the galaxy would like humans if they knew what happened?" Booker asked.

"The Toth were—no, *are* monsters," Gor'al said. "If the price to make the galaxy safe from the drones was to sacrifice them…I don't object. Nor would the Dotari. We owe the Terran Union too much."

"My parents are coming." The *gethaar* pointed in the distance.

"What?" Duke looked through his scope. "I don't see anyone."

The child let out a staccato hiss that Hoffman assumed was laughter.

"Hammers, Scipio *on approach,"* came through the IR.

"Roger, team set for pickup," Hoffman sent back as the low rumble of the ship carried through the air.

"I will leave my home," Steuben said, "to fight the Toth and Kesaht with you."

"Our next mission isn't on that front," Hoffman said. "We're going to Eridu first. They need us to—"

Steuben held up a hand. "I am in your debt. To Eridu, then I will petition to join the fight against the Kesaht. I will ask Admiral Valdar to assist my request if needed."

"Yeah…that won't be easy," Hoffman said.

"Why? Did he retire?" Steuben asked.

"Not exactly."

"Steuben," Garrison said, "why do you hate the Toth so much?"

The child put her head against Steuben's breastplate.

"Many years ago," the Karigole said as his face darkened, "the Toth were allies to my race. They raised us up from steam technology to space flight. Helped us ready our planet to fight the Xaros. We thought they were friends, blood brothers. We never learned the truth about their overlords until it was too late.

"The Toth leadership caste survive with their brains and neural systems suspended in a tank. They achieved a form of immortality by consuming the mental energy of other sentient races. And the Karigole are long-lived. Our minds proved to be too much of a temptation for them to resist.

"Once they had total control of our technology, our defenses…they conquered our world. Then they murdered us. One by one, we went to our deaths to feed the overlords.

"I was off world with my cohort of warriors, trying and failing to capture a Xaros drone. When we returned home, we found the fields of the dead…and we thought we were the last of our kind. My cohort was all males. Extinction was inevitable. So we swore to make the Toth pay for what they did until we crossed over to the land of the dead. But…"

"But?" Gor'al asked.

"But my battle brother, Lafayette, was with me on the *Breitenfeld*. We went on a mission to Nibiru to kill the leader of the Toth, one named Mentiq. There we found that he kept a small group of Karigole alive, selling them off to be eaten. We saved them, praise to the Strike Marines and Valdar for their courage.

"Earth took us in, gave us a home, and protected us from the Xaros." Steuben touched his bionic eye with his mechanical hand. "Not that Lafayette and I did not give back.

"After the Ember War, we settled here. I thought my vendetta with the Toth was answered. I was wrong. And now I will fight beside you until Bale, and every other Toth, is dead by my hand."

"Opal, sounds like you've got a challenger for the dead-enemy contest," Garrison said.

"No one beats Opal," the doughboy grumbled.

"I'm staying behind the two of them the next time we get in a fight," Max grumbled.

The *Scipio* roared overhead, slowing to a hover, kicking up dust and blinding the team.

"I love a good brownout!" Max shouted. "Makes

cleaning my gear so much more fun!"

The gale subsided and the corvette lowered its ramp.

Hoffman looked to Steuben. The Karigole was on his feet, helmet donned. The *gethaar* had vanished.

"Steuben, where'd she go?" Hoffman looked around in a near panic.

"Her parents have her. You all lack training." Steuben looked off in the distance toward the village and reached out and grasped at the air. He brought his hand to his visor and mimicked eating. "Come. Let us leave."

The Karigole locked his early-model helmet over his head and marched toward the *Scipio*. With a nod of his head, Hoffman signaled the team to follow.

The lieutenant caught up to Steuben and gave a thumbs-up to a pair of sailors on the ship's lowering ramp.

"Don't you even want to know what the mission on Eridu *is*?" Hoffman asked.

"You said you needed a hunter. That is enough."

"You don't even know what we're hunting. Perhaps there's something your people have or know that would—"

"Eridu." Steuben whacked his knuckles against the lieutenant's shoulder hard enough to upset his balance. "I know a man on Eridu. *I* am the one sought after, not any other Karigole. He knows my skills. That is what the mission demands."

"Oh…" Hoffman frowned. "And who might that be?"

"An old friend."

Steuben marched up the ramp and past the sailors, one of whom did a quick head count and then a double take at a data slate.

"Hey, Marine," the sailor said. "There's eight of you. Where's the specialist?"

"We're all Marines," King said. "Former Marines still count."

Hoffman touched his transmitter.

"Captain, we're good to lift off," he said. "Let's not overstay our welcome and eat a missile for being tardy."

Chapter 9

Hoffman and his team held on to their safety harnesses as turbulence rattled the Mule. The ship would glide smoothly, then slam against something that felt like a brick wall and shift sideways.

Moments later, it fell again, rendering them weightless.

"Ohhhh, this is not my favorite part," Max said.

"How many times do we have to do this before you learn to relax and go with it?" Garrison said. "I like it. Makes me feel funny. Like climbing the rope in gym class."

Max shook his head and held up a hand to ward off further attention. "Just leave me alone. I have my process."

"Your process better not involve blowing chow," Duke said. "Again."

"One time. You fill your helmet on one drop and—"

As turbulence rattled the Mule again, Max's cheeks puffed out and he put his hand over his mouth.

Hoffman's own stomach lurched and he noticed most of the team looked queasy. "Look at the bright side. This'll be over a lot quicker than most landings."

"Welcome to the express elevator to hell, baby!" Garrison shouted.

"Oorah!" the team replied.

"I hate that movie," Booker groaned as she squirmed beneath the iron grip of her five-point restraint harness. "It's why I didn't go Pathfinder Corps. But now look at me. On a bug hunt."

Hoffman checked the battered view screen.

The research and development division had determined that being able to see outside was important for the human psyche, but structurally, windows were a bad idea. Mules were made to be functional workhorses with as much armor as they could lift or, conversely, land. As a concession, they developed camera-fed screens that would display with reasonable resolution what was happening outside the ship.

That was a moot point, though, when dropping through a storm system. Clouds ripped by the camera and lightning flashes blinded it. Hoffman dimmed the screen to minimize the effect on his vision.

"If you're all going to be sick, perhaps it's time for me to have a dip," Gor'al said.

"Keep that filthy dip stealer away from me," Duke said. "I don't know why I ever talked him into trying tobacco. I created a monster."

Hoffman felt a sudden decrease of perceived

gravity. The effect lasted five or six seconds before the dropship impacted a cushion of air, smashing him into his seat as his safety harnesses tightened.

Alerts flashed on the screen reminding Marines to stay strapped in.

"Well, ladies and gents, this is your pilot speaking. You may have noticed we're experiencing some minor turbulence. As your pilot, I've decided to minimize the effect by taking a more direct route to our destination."

"Destination? Like the ground?" Garrison complained loudly. "What's our luck with pilots? All of them have to have jokes. Don't they send them to school for that? What I need right now is realistic information. Accurate intel on what we're doing and how soon it will be before touchdown and if said touchdown involves prayer and messing my shorts."

"Again," Booker said.

"I'm pretty sure he means we're being fired at the

ground like a bullet," Max said, turning even paler and closing his visor. Strike Marine helmets could deal with vomit. Filters would purge the liquid, but it wasn't a perfect process.

"In my medical opinion," Booker said, "you should consider Dramamine."

"Or he could stop being such a sissy," Duke said.

"That's enough," King barked. "As enlightening as all this is, you're not helping your teammate." He leaned over and jabbed Max roughly on the shoulder, which nearly made him puke. "You'll make it, buddy."

"You know what goes around comes around, right?" Max said.

Gor'al shook his head. "I don't know what is so problematic. I am not having sickness. Opal is not complaining. Why are you all losing the color in your faces and why is Max needing to move stomach fluid to the outside of his body?"

Garrison leaned as close to Gor'al as his harness would allow. "It's a really important tradition. You won't be one of us until you've puked during a drop."

"That makes me sad. I don't know that I can throw up on command."

"Well, maybe you can be taught." Garrison said. "Just watch Max to see how it's done."

Hoffman received an alert from the pilot. "All right, game time," he said to the team. "Let's get ready for touchdown and deployment."

An alert chimed on the public address system and the pilot cleared his throat. *"All right, boys and girls, this is where it gets real. I won't bore you with the technical difficulties, but thank your lucky stars and say a prayer of thanksgiving to St. Kallen that I'm flying this rig. We're coming in really hard, for reasons air traffic control refused to explain."*

The ship bumped and slipped sideways across air

turbulence several times. No one spoke for long moments.

Garrison looked around, concerned. "Is anyone else waiting for the punchline? This guy really sucks."

"Also, for the record, I do have the ability to listen to all communications on the Mule. It's my ship, after all—and your comms network slaves off mine while on board. So in answer to your question, Corporal Garrison, there is no punchline. Brace yourself."

Gravity amplified as the ship decelerated hard. Hoffman felt the short wings vibrating from the propulsor engines being reversed to push away from the surface of the planet. In technical terms, they landed soft, cushioned on gravity waves that had no actual substance. To his human perception, however, it felt like he was the nail in a hammer-and-nail situation. Or maybe he was the hammer. It was hard to tell as black spots filled his vision.

He fought to breathe, pushing air out of his lungs so he could suck it in again—the opposite of normal combat breathing. Across from him, Opal was the picture of stoicism while Max dominated the other end of the misery spectrum.

Even Gor'al looked flattened and miserable.

The landing only took a second or two—it just felt like forever. A red light flashed above the door to the cockpit, indicating the pilot was talking.

"We're down." The pilot's voice sounded strained.

"That wasn't so bad," Garrison groaned. "I've had worse. Least we're not on some frozen mountain with a long walk ahead of us."

"Are you ever going to shut up about that?" Booker asked as she slapped her harness and the straps retracted into the seat.

"Nope!" Garrison bounded out of his chair and stretched.

"Team deploy and set up security around the ship," King said.

Hoffman eased out of his chair slowly, letting King take charge of the landing. Steuben remained silent and taciturn, rivaling Opal for quiet determination.

Ground crews meandered around the landing pad, their attention focused more on the outer fence separating them from the jungle than on the ship that had just landed. None wore headsets or had the ubiquitous forearm computers.

Hoffman saw a familiar face, Colonel Heinrich Fallon from the Syracuse campaign, and felt a mixture of relief and confusion. Although the man was rough and abusive, he had kept the colonists alive on Syracuse when no one else could have. Had things gone differently, Hoffman and the Dotari Armor might've been saving a planet full of slaughtered civilians and the small garrison of Marines that had been there instead of a city's worth of survivors.

As much as he respected the man—the man whose

nephew he had killed in a grisly Xaros drone incident—he knew this wasn't going to be an easy assignment. He was starting to think that Colonel Fallon was a kindred spirit he'd always find in the worst corner of the war against the Kesaht.

The colonel had a pistol in a thigh holster, not the standard-issue gauss sidearm Strike Marine officers normally carried. Hoffman couldn't place the make and model at first glance, and it nagged the lieutenant that Fallon wore simple fatigues, instead of the Corps' iconic power armor.

"Look sharp," Hoffman said.

"Any reason why we had to do the combat drop?" Garrison asked. "I'm just asking because I'm worried about Max. He looks awful…and no one's dressed for combat around here."

"I'm sure there's a rational explanation." Hoffman approached the colonel and saluted. Fallon returned the salute smartly, then told them to stand at ease.

"It's an honor to meet you, Steuben," Fallon said to the Karigole. "I've heard a lot about you from the locals."

Hoffman was surprised the colonel hadn't commented on the Karigole's old armor. Fallon was a stickler for details and didn't tolerate shabby equipment. Hoffman noticed many other people in the ground security forces giving Steuben and Gor'al strange looks. That he was leading a team with members of two different alien races and one of the last doughboys in service had not given him any sense of being more elite than all-human teams. If anything, he thought they looked like a motley crew.

"Orders, sir?" King asked.

"Take the rest of the team to the quartermaster for new equipment. Draw gear for Steuben and Hoffman—they're with me—and make it fast. It'll be sundown soon."

"New gear. Yes, sir," King said, giving Hoffman a

quick look. "I have your specs, sir. Not Steuben's."

"Won't matter, Gunney. Get it done." Fallon turned and walked away, catching Hoffman flat-footed.

The colonel retrieved a short, chewed-up cigar from his utility pocket and stuck it in the corner of his mouth. From what Hoffman remembered, Fallon didn't like to have his orders questioned. At the same time, he didn't like mindless sheep either.

Once they were away from the officers, Garrison and Max began arguing, their voices easily carrying across the unusually silent airfield. Duke seemed to think he didn't need the re-equip, because his equipment was custom fit to his role as a sniper. King threatened a long, arduous run around the base to learn the lay of the land.

Steuben, Hoffman, and Fallon watched them for a moment.

"Combat landing wasn't pleasant, I know, but it's damn necessary on Eridu," Fallon said.

Hoffman waited, knowing the colonel would continue.

"We can't have aircraft exposed for too long over the city. It's a significant safety risk. Just leave it at that. All will be explained in the formal briefing and mission planning. The colony chief likes to be involved in that sort of thing, but he's not bad for a civilian—probably because he's a former Corpsman and spent enough time with Strike Marines to get the Navy scrubbed off him." He looked again at Steuben. "I appreciate having another hero of the Ember War. Wasn't exactly sure we'd get you here, but Hoffman has a reputation for pulling off tough missions."

Except when the Breitenfeld *gets captured right out from under us,* Hoffman thought.

Steuben growled in the back of his throat but said nothing. He towered over Hoffman, which made him a giant compared to the colonel.

"I cannot speak to hearsay," the Karigole said.

Fallon chuckled. "I have it on good authority all the scenes starring you in that *Last Stand on Takeni* movie weren't entirely factual."

Steuben spat on the ground.

Fallon gripped the cigar between the base of two fingers and removed it from his mouth.

"I looked into Adams. Can the Karigole hear this?" the colonel asked.

"Yes, sir," Hoffman said.

"Fair enough. Corporal Adams was transferred to Ulysses Tholis crater on Mars. Orders signed by the commandant himself."

"Mars, sir? Can't say I'm familiar with every last spot."

"Let's keep the 'sir' calling under control when away from troops and civilians," Fallon said, exhaling smoke. "Speeds up talk. As for Tholis, I'd never heard of it either. I'm not a fan of not knowing, so I looked into it.

Wish I hadn't—the intel boys slapped me on the pee-pee pretty hard."

"That's…odd," Hoffman said, pondering the information. "We're already cleared for black ops."

"Intel weenies call it 'sensitive compartmentalized information' for a reason. Just because you're cleared for one info stovepipe don't mean you're cleared for all of them. There's more."

Hoffman waited, hoping to learn more about this mission and why it was so important.

"There's been mass personnel transfer from across the military," Fallon said. "I'm pretty sure at least some of my problems on Syracuse came from that shit show. I've been in a long time, and I've seen my share of disorganization and suffered under the command of staff officers with no clue as to what type of personnel we need in the field. But this is different. The sheer scope of the transfers is stunning. No rhyme or reason. And they all went to that crater."

Hoffman grappled with the new information but didn't have an explanation. He wasn't about to float his own conspiracy theories in front of the senior Marine.

Fallon continued. "I've got a contact on the Mars orbital watch. He sent me this." He reached into a pocket and pulled out a photograph. Hoffman took the picture, feeling like he was in a museum as he held the obsolete bit of technology, wondering why the colonel didn't just use his tablet.

The picture showed a cracked dome fit over a crater on the red planet.

"It looks abandoned," Hoffman said. "How recent is this?"

Fallon nodded. "Days old. That's all I've got."

"Then where's Adams? Why ship people from all over the Union to this spot then abandon it?" Hoffman wasn't sure if these revelations were better than having no information. The colonel's demeanor wasn't reassuring.

"Like I said, that's all I have. And getting that out of Mars was a feat in and of itself. Planet's locked down tighter than proper ladies in a port when a ship pulls in for liberty. Adams is your Marine. I respect you trying to keep up on her, but I don't know what to tell you." He motioned them toward a ground car and waited for them to get in, then went to the driver's side and got behind the wheel.

"We're taking this car? It has a tailpipe. It's not even electric. They drive antiques on Eridu?"

The colonel chewed on his cigar and started the vehicle. As the engine turned over and the pistons rumbled, Hoffman felt like he was in an old movie.

"Yep."

"Why?" Hoffman flinched at his familiar tone and added, "Sir."

"I'll let that one go, but control yourself. I work for a living. 'Sir' me again, I'll cancel your block leave."

"My team's getting block leave?"

"No. Life is suffering, Hoffman. Ancient Buddhist saying."

"Yes…uh, Colonel. Why are we taking this old ground car?"

"It beats walking," Fallon said, trying three times to get the car in gear.

"Is it supposed to make that grinding noise?" Steuben asked.

Fallon jammed the stick shift forward, flexing the muscles in his forearm, grunting in satisfaction as he finally rammed it home. "I'd never driven a stick before last week. Give me a break."

He pulled shakily away from the curb, the vehicle lurching twice.

"Why start now?" Hoffman asked, grabbing the safety handle on the side door with one hand.

"I wouldn't have to do this myself if all the kids

hadn't been evacuated off world. They like driving these things. Eridu is red space…high chance of Kesaht attack. Most noncombatants are gone. The rest are still here because of what I'm about to show you."

Hoffman shook his head. "Sir, what does that have to do with ground cars and unnecessary combat drops?"

"The Beast keeps us from using the city's auto-drive network. It generates an energy field around it that indiscriminately shuts down electronics. Flying over the city results in flying into the ground."

"A beast does all this? It doesn't seem like something an animal could manage—or would even be concerned about. You're telling me this creature has somehow set out to strategically sabotage the auto-drive network?"

Fallon bounced the car off a curb, then overcorrected. It was a slight movement, but compared to auto-drive maneuvers, it seemed like they were on a roller coaster. "You'll see."

"If we get there alive," Steuben said.

Colonel Fallon drove along hastily constructed fences topped with razor wire that looked like prison walls. The heavy-duty chain link and coils of sharpened death on top of it gleamed in the dying sunset.

"Those won't hold back the Kesaht," Hoffman said. He was surprised the colonel who had fought the Kesaht so fiercely on Syracuse would tolerate such poor defenses.

"That's not for them; that's for the Beast. Quick fix. Hasn't been tested yet but makes people feel better."

Chapter 10

Gunney King respected quartermasters. That didn't mean he liked them or enjoyed their company.

"Say again?" he asked, his right hand on the verge of forming a knife shape.

The quartermaster stood like an oak tree, hands clasped behind his back. "Is this what Strike Marines do these days? Question orders? Let me see if I expressed the wishes of Colonel Fallon accurately." He looked at a clipboard. "Yep, that's what I thought I said. You must remove all Mark 9 power armor and pack it in these crates. The same with gauss weapons and all other gear."

"I'm not a big fan of fighting naked. The lieutenant can pull off a leather thong, but the rest of us are mere mortals," Garrison said. "Just because I'm a powerlifter doesn't mean my muscles are bulletproof."

"You're a dork," Booker muttered.

"Hostile work environment," Garrison shot back.

One of the quartermaster's assistants rolled in a table stacked with neatly folded combat fatigues. Boots lined the lower rack and backpacks, belts, and gloves were assembled in the assigned gear in a grayish-tan camouflage pattern.

King resisted the powerful urge to go toe-to-toe with the quartermaster. They were equivalent rank, but the man had the home-court advantage and the legitimacy of being right. Orders were orders.

"You heard the man. Let's get it done, team." He removed his armor and catalogued every piece of gear down to the contents of the last utility pouch, then did the same with his weapons, packing each neatly into the crates. It felt like he was going on a long trip or perhaps retiring from service.

"Please use the insulation and cushioning layer," the quartermaster said. "They're prefabricated but can be modified to fit the small idiosyncrasies of your individual load-outs. I don't want your stuff getting banged up if we have to ship it through the pneumatic tube network."

"The pneumonia what?" Garrison asked. "Speak English. I don't have my language translator anymore."

"An embarrassing, stupid dork," Booker said. "Please stop talking."

The quartermaster, unfazed by the exchange, stepped toward a wall and aimed a knife hand at a thick network of insulated pipes on the ceiling. "Weird tech from the first colonists. They brought it from some alien planet. It works. We don't complain."

"I bet Gor'al would fit in one," Garrison said.

"I am—how do Marines say it—game. Down with it. Good to go. Opal, lift me into the tube," the Dotari said.

"That's enough," King said. "Don't put him in there."

The quartermaster, his face growing redder by the second, locked his hands behind his back and stood at modified parade rest. "Some junior Marines tried it and lived. Though after the colonel got wind of the stunt, they wished they'd suffocated."

Garrison patted the quartermaster on the shoulder. "But we're *Strike* Marines. We'd turn it into a rollercoaster of fun."

The quartermaster looked at Garrison like he'd grown three heads.

King knew he should dress the breacher down but decided to let it pass.

"So…" Garrison said to the quartermaster, "we getting new stuff? Maybe some special, cutting-edge prototypes that make armor look old school? I'd really like a jet pack and a laser gauntlet if you have one."

The quartermaster removed Garrison's hand and stepped back. "You will all be issued new equipment. No jet packs or other toys. Strictly analog."

Two corporals wheeled in racks full of weapons—simple assault rifles with iron sights and none of the bells and whistles of their gauss rifles. The quartermaster and his crew assigned each of them an assault rifle and a similarly low-tech sidearm.

Duke received an old-style, bolt-action sniper rifle with a lensed scope fixed to it.

"Wow, that's impressive. I haven't seen one of these for a while." Duke picked it up and examined it after doing a series of safety checks, his expert's touch clear to everyone. "I've always wanted to have one of these old relics for my personal arsenal."

"Wouldn't everyone," the quartermaster said dryly,

putting more distance between himself and Garrison.

"When you're done with the mission, I'll have a series of forms you can complete. Should it be approved, it can be shipped to your base of operation."

Duke looked at him. "Why the sour look?"

"You're making a lot of work for me," the quartermaster said.

"That's what we do," Duke said with a big smile.

The quartermaster reached for Ice Claw, Duke's sniper rifle he had carried since Koen, the winter world.

Duke snatched up the weapon and retreated a step, holding it close to his body with his right hand and fending off the quartermaster with his left. "Hold on there, dude. That's a good way to get throat-punched. What makes you think you can touch Ice Claw?"

"I can touch it because you didn't follow instructions. The instructions were to pack it into the crate. If you won't pack it, then I'll pack it. Are these orders unclear? Am I speaking a foreign language?" The quartermaster went on without waiting for an answer. "There will be no active electronics on this planet. None on your weapon, none on your communications device, no electronics. Is that one hundred percent clear?"

"Whoa!" Garrison exclaimed. "I'm a breacher! You can't take ignition boxes. It's not safe. What about my decryption software? Doors don't open themselves."

Max pushed ahead of him. "How exactly do I run comms without electronic hardware? We're not getting stuck on this godforsaken planet with no way to phone home. You going to issue me a carrier pigeon?"

"Not yet. They're being trained," one of the quartermasters said.

Booker looked as though she also had a list of arguments, but she only shook her head and clenched her teeth.

"Listen up, Hammers," King shouted. "You have

your orders. Do I need to reinforce them? We know Colonel Fallon doesn't play games. Quit gold-bricking and get it together. Improvise. Adapt. Overcome."

"Oorah," the team responded grudgingly.

The quartermaster glared at King. "Colonel Fallon saved this colony from anarchy soon as he got on the ground. He knows what the hell he's doing."

"Saw him do the same thing on Syracuse," King said. "But just what we're supposed to do here with our Karigole friend and gear that looks like it came out of the jungles of Vietnam to help the colonel is still a bit nebulous."

A tense moment passed. "They didn't tell you about the Beast?" the quartermaster said in a half whisper.

"The details are fuzzy," King said.

"I suggest you and your Devil Dogs get familiar with your equipment before nightfall. That's when the Beast comes for us." The man looked out the window to the late afternoon sky and swallowed hard.

"Fair enough." King and the quartermaster nodded unofficial salutes and parted. "Bring it in," King said to his team.

Sensing his mood, the team gathered around him, new uniforms and rifles clutched in their arms.

"Get your gear on," King said. "You're all Strike Marines and you had to earn your power armor by busting your ass in fatigues just like you've got now. We're going to the range to qualify on these weapons."

"No floating dot optics," Max said, "no laser designators, no onboard ballistic computers…" He looked over at Duke. "Some of us will struggle."

"You want to make a bet on that one, sparky?" Duke spat dip into a plastic bottle.

Garrison pulled the bolt back on his new rifle and peered into the breach. "I'm still not sold on this idea—no disrespect, Gunney," Garrison said. "Do these things require actual lubricant?"

"Gun oil," Booker said. "You make it sound dirty."

"Like Duke's girlfriends," Max said.

"Duke has a girlfriend with dirty oil?" Gor'al asked.

"Hard to explain, Gor. I'll take you to the Chrome Pole when we get back to Phoenix. It'll be life-changing," Duke said, caressing the old sniper rifle.

"I know the colonists here are from some sort of Akkadian background," Booker said. "But this feels like we're going to fight a war against the Society of Creative Anachronism."

"Armor are the ones with the swords, not Strike Marines," Max said.

"I thought those were ceremonial," Gor'al said, "then I saw my own people's armor fighting the Kesaht." His quills bristled slightly. "I would rather be shot than stabbed. I attribute this to a genetic fear of being eaten."

"Guess humans and Dotari aren't all that different,"

Duke said.

"Yeah, might as well be throwing rocks." Garrison shook his head woefully. "I mean, iron sights, really?"

"It's funny you mention that. Everyone get ready for some range time. We'll start qualifications like you're raw recruits—just to be sure we don't have any hidden deficiencies," King said.

Duke held up a bullet and sniffed it. "This has a chemical propellant. We're living history now."

Gor'al was even more mystified than the Strike Marines. "At least you have had basic familiarization training with these crude things." He locked back the slide to his assault rifle and snapped his finger in the breach. "I am not understanding how this works."

"We'll walk you through it," King said. "Maybe they've got equipment for dime and washer drills."

****

Hoffman and Steuben followed Colonel Fallon into the command center. The entrance was framed by a blast door. Farther inside were another set of doors to underground bunkers.

"Are we expecting an air raid?" Hoffman asked, doing a double take as a man with an intricately braided beard that hung down to the center of his chest walked past them.

Fallon shook his head. "No, it's worse than that. We started moving into the bunkers a few days ago. Takes time. A lot of our gear wasn't made to be moved and a lot of people are resisting the idea of locking themselves underground. Every time the Beast rips up a building, the locals see more wisdom in my plan, but it's a work in progress. We'll keep operations above ground for now."

Fallon led them through a hallway to the main room, returning salutes as he passed guards and other military personnel.

In the center of the command room was a scale model of the city. Although the detail was impressive, it seemed clunky compared to holographic briefing tables and high-resolution flat screens Hoffman was accustomed to.

"What's that smell? It's masking every other scent," Steuben asked, tilting his head back and flaring his nostrils.

"Lavender candles. Yarrow's wife and a few of the other women claim it has a calming effect." Fallon shrugged. "And we need the light. Torches build up too much smoke."

As they walked, Steuben leaned close to Hoffman and said, "Despite the lavender abomination, I can still smell the fear in the room."

Hoffman nodded in agreement.

Fallon spoke with several of his personnel and then aimed a knife hand at a man facing away from them. "This is Yarrow, my second-in-command. His predecessor…died unexpectedly."

"I think you have the chain of command backward. I'm the colony chief now, remember?" the man said as he turned around. He had medical corps insignia on his shoulders and a nonregulation goatee with beads worked into it. A wry smile spread across his face and he pointed at the Karigole.

Hoffman frowned as he studied the doctor. Something about him was familiar.

The doctor spread his arms out wide and came toward the alien. "Steuben!"

"Yarrow? Did you glue that mass of human crotch-growth to your face?" The Karigole's eyes went wide as the colony chief gave him a big hug, trying to avoid smashing his face into Steuben's but failing. They drew back and awkwardly patted each other on the back.

"Same old Steuben," Yarrow said.

Suddenly, Hoffman realized where he'd seen

Yarrow before—the Ember War–era propaganda film, *Last Stand on Takeni*. This was the same Yarrow that served with Hale on the *Breitenfeld*.

"You have progressed well beyond adolescence," Steuben growled pleasantly. "How old are you now? Twelve?"

Yarrow stepped back, stroking his goatee. "I feel my age in my knees and hips. You know how long it took me to grow this? I got sick of my wife's people thinking I was a woman the first time they met me."

Hoffman observed the soldiers and civilians in the room, noting their distinctive facial hair. While Yarrow, a man Steuben apparently knew, had a reasonable goatee, the rest of the local personnel had epic braided beards that often ran high onto their cheekbones. No delineation between sideburns and beards existed. He'd seen something like the style in history books but couldn't remember where exactly. His guess was this was a historical or traditional style of Akkadians, the heritage the people of Eridu identified with.

"Colonel, we distributed the flares to the sentry posts," a soldier reported to Fallon.

"Better to head toward flares than trying to figure out which way gunfire's coming from in the middle of the night," the colonel said. Darting his eyes between Yarrow and Steuben, he added, "Now that we're done with Old Home Week?"

"We'll catch up later," Yarrow said as he picked up a pencil and made a mark on a sheet of paper.

"Did you require hormone supplements to grow that?" Steuben asked.

"I knew you wouldn't change," Yarrow said. "You're still a master hunter? Or did easy living on Nimrod take away that edge?"

"Your Earth humor is not appreciated. Tell me of my prey," the Karigole said.

"*We* are the prey." Yarrow pressed a series of buttons. "I'm activating the holo screen. Pay attention because I can only do this once before we go into mandatory shutdown. This is an exception to protocol 585." He looked around the room for confirmation. Colonel Fallon nodded quickly.

"Proceeding with the presentation," Yarrow said, starting the video as holo screens formed over the scale model of the city. Hoffman recognized helmet-camera footage from power armor, but the figures moving in the screen wore slimmer gear than Strike Marine standard. Men and women moved slowly and methodically through an alien structure. Hoffman bit his tongue at their technique, but these weren't Strike Marines—they were Pathfinders. The Terran Union's scouting and exploration corps didn't have the same combat training as he and his Marines.

"Is this on Eridu?" Hoffman asked.

"Yes." Yarrow's tone suggested that interruptions weren't appreciated. A sense of urgency filled the room as the holo played.

The Pathfinders advanced using hand signals, sweeping the area with their infrared lights on their weapons. Hoffman knew that without the video feeds, they would be in pitch-blackness. The infrared flashlights were only visible with the enhanced optics of the operators' equipment and their cameras. The recording scanned over dead alien specimens floating in tanks filled with murky liquid. As the Pathfinders moved into a larger room, they saw a tangle of snakelike creatures suspended in some sort of stasis.

Massive doors lined one of the walls. The area was so large that Hoffman thought it looked like elephants or rhinoceroses could be used to play polo in one section of the underground complex.

Yarrow and the others shifted uneasily as static

snapped through the holo for a second.

"I'm going to fast-forward through this part," Yarrow said. "There are several instances of this static. The Pathfinders start to get really nervous and there are arguments about going back—not something you normally hear from them. They're almost as gung ho as Strike Marines."

Fallon shook his head. "Negative. I want them to get at least one uncut view of the sequence of events. They might see something we missed."

"*We've come far enough. Let's come back with more firepower,*" a voice said.

"*Negative. There's nothing down here but dead things,*" the team leader said then activated his comm channel. "*Away Team One for Command, we've found remnants of the planet's lost civilization. Looks like the place has degraded since the Xaros stasis fields have collapsed. Doc, can you give me a reading?*"

Another Pathfinder spoke up. "*I'm guessing about two decades. There's a slow decay that's very unusual…*"

The video went fuzzy for a second. The Pathfinders discussed the interference briefly but moved on as though it had already happened once or twice during their exploration.

"*I really don't like this shit, boss,*" a voice said.

"*Grow a pair. Or do you want to go back to the Strike Marines? It's safer, I hear.*"

"*Ha ha, that's a good one. Can I at least bring a big gun next time? Maybe some real armor?*"

Screams came over the channel and the Pathfinders took cover. The shouting ended in a wet cough.

Shadows moved, briefly overloading the team's infrared optics. The head of a Pathfinder sprang off his shoulders and the camera view tumbled. For a moment, Hoffman was disoriented as the video view spun. When it stopped, he saw the Pathfinder's feet. A second later, the body rocked and fell, blood spurting from the neck. The recording cut out.

Yarrow exhaled slowly. "That's the last thing we got from the team." He turned off the recording. With careful movements, he removed a folder full of high-resolution photographs. Hoffman had rarely seen actual printed photos in the age of digital tablets, heads-up visor displays, and holographic projections. A technician pulled out a battery pack from beneath the terrain model.

Yarrow continued. "Our best guess is the Beast was some sort of experiment trapped in Xaros stasis for nearly a thousand years. The Pathfinders woke it up."

"And how is this Beast responsible for all these new protocols and why we had to give up our gear?" Hoffman said.

"It's attracted to electricity," Yarrow said. "We figured that out after we lost several security teams in the jungle. That's why I had to keep that video short. The Beast also disrupts powered tech—your armor would lock up when the Beast gets within a few hundred yards, leaving you to be a nice snack with a candy shell when it catches up to you. Any power source becomes a beacon for the Beast, which is why the city's operating on candles and hydrocarbon tech we can power off completely. We can't explain how the Beast is generating the disruption field."

Yarrow showed them pictures of crashed drones. "Anything that flies within line of sight gets fried. Anything that moves within a bubble of a few hundred meters of the Beast goes down…or the Beast wrecks it. We don't have any recordings of the Beast, just the aftermath of its attacks." He pointed at the ceiling. "We've fabricated a few lights that run off chemo luminescence—the mother of all glow-stick networks, essentially. But that's limited. Most of the city is on candle and oil lamps. We'll risk electricity during the day if there's no sign of the Beast, otherwise we'd be making our coffee over a fire, Saint

Kallen preserve us. Also, Steuben I need you to shut off your cybernetics. Sorry."

"To hunt a worthy prey with one eye and one hand," Steuben removed his false eye and plucked out the battery pack. He bent his cyborg hand into a slight grip and yanked a small box from the bottom servos. "This will be a tale sung around the fires for years."

"And I thought you were a fatalist," Hoffman said. "This Beast is a…tactical problem. No gauss weapons. No power armor. No comms network…and we don't know what it looks like. There anything else you can tell us?"

"It doesn't eat what it kills," Yarrow said. "I autopsied the bodies. No sign of any feeding."

"Animals kill for territory and for hunger," Steuben said, "not for pleasure. The Xaros passed over this world, built the Crucible jump gate. If they encountered a living civilization, they would have erased all trace of it. The civilization here must have been extinct when the Xaros arrived. What do you know of the original inhabitants?"

"Nothing." Yarrow shook his head. "Original survey of Eridu showed the place was uninhabited. We did LIDAR scans after some artifacts were uncovered during the city's expansion, and there are cities out there buried under thousands of years' worth of jungle growth. That's how we found the underground lab not too far away."

"Could the Beast have been meant as a weapon against the Xaros?" Steuben asked. "Something purpose-bred to fight their drones?"

"That's our working hypothesis," Yarrow said.

"Were you able to recover the Pathfinders?"

"We lost nearly fifty Marines trying to get to the artifact site," Colonel Fallon answered. "Then the Beast showed up on our doorstep. Ripped apart three battery sinks and killed another dozen personnel before we started shutting everything off at night. Started using what the troops called low-tech glow rocks and other kid stuff to see at night. Back to the fire age on Eridu. If it weren't for combustion-engine-powered vehicles and the pneumatic tubes, nothing would get moved around here."

"It prefers to strike at night," Yarrow said. "We run critical systems for short periods during the day—hospitals, sewage, and fuel transfer stations mostly. Radar and sonar scans. Colonel Fallon puts his people on high alert and we take care of business as quickly as possible. It's quite a production."

"Show me the Beast," Steuben demanded. "You must have something."

"I would if I could, but every camera or streaming device that gets within the disruption bubble gets fried," Yarrow said as he selected one of the print pictures and held it up to display a footprint: an oval pad with four fingers of varying length. "I can't find a species on Eridu that matches this track or is as territorial. No local creatures disrupt electricity or show any sensitivity to it."

Steuben examined the picture. "The claw patterns are wrong. Asymmetry is always a sign of genetic inferiority. This Beast could not mate. Could it have been brought in from off world?"

"That's our second hypothesis." Yarrow shrugged. "We don't have data from neighboring systems and the original Eridu population didn't leave any sign they had space travel."

"What does it matter?" Fallon asked. "It's here. It's killing our people. It needs to be dealt with."

"Why is this planet still occupied?" Hoffman asked. He knew the colonel's experience on Syracuse and expected the man to be more careful with civilian populations after that world had nearly been wiped out by the Kesaht.

A grim silence spread over the room. Yarrow picked up another photo of a screen capture from a Pathfinder camera. It displayed a triangle the size of a basketball glowing with black bands around it. Hoffman felt a chill at the sight of it.

"We found this in a message buffer, flagged critical. Do you know what it is?" Yarrow asked.

"Qa'Resh technology. The Ibarras have been after that. They've got a thing for archaeotech sites," Hoffman said.

"Every species in the galaxy is after Qa'Resh tech," Fallon said. "That's why we're still here. Earth wants that device. If the former occupants studied it and used it to make something as powerful as the Beast…it could be valuable to our own war efforts."

Steuben growled in the back of his throat. "But we have to get through the Beast first. The device is in its lair. This is a behavior we can use for the hunt."

"That's why we asked for you, Steuben," Yarrow said. "Hunting something like this with only low-tech devices…" He looked at Fallon, who crossed his arms over his chest and looked away. "We've had nothing but failure. Bloody, awful failure. Lost too many good men."

"The Beast attacks at night?" Steuben asked.

Yarrow nodded. "Mostly."

"Then I will track it myself. Kill it myself. I will send its head back as a gift to the *gethaar*, then my hunt will continue."

An awkward silence filled the room as though the Karigole warrior had just said he was going to fly into the sun.

"Lieutenant Hoffman, Steuben, we have a technical expert waiting for you in the next room," Colonel Fallon said. "Let's not rush to failure."

****

A thousand thoughts ran through Hoffman's mind as he left the briefing area and entered a smaller side room.

The technical expert proved to be a small Asian woman with a metal brace on her right arm. He tried not to stare as the prosthetic moved the weakened limb for her. A bright pucker of scar tissue at the base of her skull caught his attention.

"Hello, Lieutenant," she said with a half-smile. "I'm Dr. Masako. Well, I'm still a resident, but it's easier than saying Junior Doc Masako. Or Almost Doc Masako. Patients don't like being treated by someone still on probation."

"Thomas Hoffman, good to meet you," he said, proffering his hand and immediately regretting it.

The brace on her arm creaked as the metal exoskeleton jerked her arm forward. He shook a clammy hand, one that did not grasp his in return.

"Sorry," Hoffman said. "I didn't mean to—"

"Locals don't shake," she said, and her arm swung back down to her side. "It's fine. Need all the practice I can get for the neural shunts in between power lockdowns."

"Shunts?" Hoffman raised an eyebrow. "I thought that tech was obsolete."

"It is, unless you burn out a section of your nervous system." She touched the scar at the base of her skull with her other hand. "Armor. Almost. Managed to get my plugs and walk on Mars, then my body rejected the implant in a spectacular fashion. I tell myself I was lucky, could've redlined and spent my last days as a vegetable."

"Sorry to hear that," Hoffman said.

She reached out and back with her braced arm. "Few more months and the shunts will have remapped the pathways. Then I can get a transplant. Or that was the plan until the Beast showed up and screwed up my sync time."

"Then let us get on with the hunt," Steuben said.

"Oh, wow…you're scarier in person than Yarrow let on," Masako said. "Thought you'd be taller after seeing you in that movie."

Steuben let out a low growl and Hoffman held up a hand to signal her to drop the topic.

Masako laughed nervously and swept a hand over a table filled with matte-black equipment. "Take a look, yes? What you see here are cameras. Did you know you can capture high-resolution images using light-sensitive film? No digitization or electricity needed. Strictly windup."

"It's like the early twentieth century around here," Hoffman answered. "Before Edison."

"It's our analog solution to getting a picture of the Beast. The colonel has people setting them up around the city. Your team will need to know how to operate them. Watch closely," she said.

He stepped to the table and put his hands on it, directing all his attention to her lesson. Her soft voice made him wonder how she'd managed to get so far into the armor program before washing out. A decent bedside manner wasn't a trait he imagined for the brutal soldiers plugged into killing machines.

"This is the latch. Undo it, open it, and look here. Don't pull the film out to look at it or you'll ruin it. This cylinder goes here, and you pull out the film and hook it to these tiny teeth. Do you see how the gear advances the film?"

"That seems…fragile," Hoffman said.

"It's ridiculous and archaic," she said, laughing. "If you Strike Marines can manage not to break it, it'll help the war effort."

"Have you ever met Strike Marines?" Hoffman asked.

"We have these all over the city, some of them with mechanical triggers," she said. "Hard to know your enemy if you don't know what it even looks like."

Hoffman tried to imagine the Beast stepping on a pressure plate and cameras and flashbulbs going off. The image from an old movie made him chuckle.

"I should warn you that the film is extremely flammable. What's so funny?"

"Nothing; just imagined it at a photo shoot," Hoffman said. "Thanks for the warning about the fire risk."

She handed him a small clip-on camera. "For your helmet."

"This is a camera?"

She twisted a key on the side of the small device and clicking filled the room.

"Too much noise," Steuben said.

"Just turn it on after the shooting starts," Masako said. "That isn't very helpful or comforting, I know. We sent requirements for a better device back to Earth, but with the war, I doubt our request is a priority. This is the best we can manage."

Hoffman looked out the window and saw a flare go off against the twilight. It arced through the sky, rising higher and higher until it began its descent.

Masako shifted nervously and flipped a switch on her exoskeleton. Her arm went limp against her side.

"Where's that?" Hoffman asked.

"The supply depot," she said as a siren wailed in the distance.

Hoffman called his team on the radio, cringing apologetically for using the technology when Masako frowned at him. "I have to be able to talk to my team." He directed them to meet him at the supply depot.

Locking him with an unusually intense stare that reminded him of a cross between a gunnery sergeant and a stern professor, she stepped close. "Radio use is up to you, but dangerous. Don't think you've somehow found a safe zone where it can be used. Now, for one more thing you're not going to like."

She pulled Hoffman's emergency tab on his armor and it fell off. She stepped to a pallet of gear and opened a carbon-fiber crate. Inside was analog gear that looked heavy and unpowered. "Get changed," she said. Then she began to remove her arm brace with a wince of pain as the unsupported limb flopped to her side.

"I…OK, this will be interesting. Thanks for the warning about radio traffic. I won't forget."

"Radio conversations—on any frequency—are a luxury, so don't beat around the bush."

"Command for Hammer One," a voice said in his earpiece. "We've got a situation."

Hoffman responded with the mic click, mindful of Masako's warning about attracting the Beast. "We need your team to respond to the attack site at the supply depot."

"Understood," Hoffman said. He pinged King's radio. "Did you get the call to respond to the site of the attack?"

"Yes, sir," King said. "We're on the way. We got new gear, which is not what I want to wear in a fight. Doubt complaining will get us our stuff back."

"Yeah, I've got mine. 'Interesting' is one way to describe it." He returned to the command room and found Steuben and Yarrow arguing over the scale model of the city.

Locals gathered around, listening with worried expressions. Hoffman nudged his way through the crowd of soldiers, civilians, and scientists.

"I can set up a trap, if you'll give me resources," Steuben explained.

Yarrow shook his head. "Too many civilians in that sector. We're not bait."

"Steuben, we've got a call," Hoffman interrupted. "There's been an attack on the supply depot. The team's already en route."

"Then why are we having useless arguments with bureaucrats?" Steuben pointed an accusing finger at Yarrow.

"I might resemble that remark, but that doesn't mean

I'm wrong," Yarrow said. "You're lucky I like you—and know you might eat my face—or I'd tell you how to do your job."

"You have learned much, young one," Steuben said. "I will credit your wife for your mature outlook."

"She'd like to see you again," Yarrow said.

Steuben gave Hoffman the onceover as they left the room. "I like your new-not-new gear."

"Really?"

"No. I joke. Have you formed a plan to kill the Beast?" Steuben asked.

Hoffman pulled a handful of small cameras from his utility pouch and showed them to the Karigole. "I think these will help."

"Now *you* joke. What are those? Death rays?"

"Cameras."

The Karigole curled back his upper lip. "Are you going to capture an image of the Beast and taunt it to death on social media?"

"Well, if you don't see it, kill it, skin it, and eat it tonight, then maybe we can gather some intelligence that'll be useful later," Hoffman said.

"Reasonable," Steuben muttered.

Hoffman put away the cameras and ran street to street until he saw his team moving toward the flare site. Their routes converged.

"Radio silent," Hoffman said as he accepted a low-tech assault rifle and several magazines of ammo. He slapped one into the weapon and frowned at the single switch on the side.

"Have to pull the charging handle to get one in the chamber," King said. "Not an autoloader like our gauss. Gas power cycles rounds. You can fire on semiautomatic or three-round bursts."

"Oh…" Hoffman's face went red as he racked the charging handle. "How…quaint."

"Bullets pack a hell of a kick," King said. "Like a .30-06 my grandpa had. Meant to take down something big."

Hoffman looked down at his fatigues and grimaced. This was how Marines had gone into a fight since the first days of the old United States Marine Corps. He'd make do without power armor.

"Nothing to do now but improvise, adapt, and overcome," Hoffman said as shots rang in the distance. The rattling staccato of the weapons was surreal, like being in an old movie as the sun dropped toward the horizon.

He handed out cameras. "Everybody, take one of these, attach them to your armor where they won't get blocked when you aim weapons, then let's get a defensive perimeter in place."

Booker took the first camera. "How cute," she said dryly.

"Are we getting our gear from cereal boxes now?"

Garrison asked.

"Might as well," Hoffman said. "These are analog tech. They require film. Treat them as fragile and keep in mind that they're loud. You start taking pictures when you're trying to stay hidden, you might have problems."

Duke pulled back from the mini-camera handout. "I won't be needing one of those."

"Take one," King said. "We'll get you fitted with a telescopic lens at some point. But for now, take what's offered."

"He's not taking one," Duke said, nodding at Steuben.

"They are too noisy," the Karigole said.

Duke spread his hands as though to indicate "You see?"

"We need a good look at one of these things. The best chance is for us to catch a long-range camera shot. For that, you're going to need a big lens. Think of it as a kinder, gentler sniper rifle," Hoffman said.

"Yes, sir." Duke spat out his tobacco wad.

"But that's in the future. Our immediate objective is to travel to the supply depot, contact and destroy the enemy if the opportunity arises, and secure the zone to make it safe for civilians and other personnel," Hoffman said. "King, let's move out."

The sun was below the horizon now, casting a purplish glow out of the city with a thin strip of orange along the horizon. Something roared in the distance.

"Sounds like a Beast to me," Garrison said.

"A dominance call," Steuben said. "But that makes little sense."

"Why? Apex predators will do apex predatory things, right?" Max asked.

"There are no others of its kind on this planet," Steuben said. "Establishing dominance is useless if there's nothing to dominate."

"Maybe there's more than one out there," Duke said.

"Bro, come on," Garrison said. "Don't jinx us."

"Food for thought. Garrison, take point," Hoffman said. "King and Gor'al, bring up the rear. Keep a perimeter."

"And look up," Steuben said. "Always be looking up."

Without power, the city was darker than it should have been, but lanterns and candles showed the rough outline of buildings and streets in the distance. As true darkness descended upon the city, the glow lights managed to heighten just how off the situation on Eridu was, like the team had traveled back in time to fight a demon of legend.

"I've got a bad feeling about this," Garrison said.

The team moved as silently as possible through the abandoned streets.

"What? No one's going to argue with me? No shit-talking?" Garrison asked at a half whisper. The crack of assault rifles carried down the street.

"Oh, me! I was to talk of the shit." Gor'al bounced up on his toes in his excitement, which made him seem almost as though he were skipping forward with his assault rifle carried at port arms. "Don't be scared, sissy. You're like a little girl!"

Booker grabbed him by the chin strap on his armor and calmed his bouncy step. "Settle down there, Gor. It's not the time for that."

Mortars fired parachute flares high into the air. The lights swung and cast weird shadows as they descended over the city.

"For once, I agree with Garrison," Max said.

King put a hand on Garrison's shoulder to stop him as the team froze, weapons ready. He motioned his palm toward the ground and everybody took a knee. An explosion of activity left an alleyway, quickly resolving into the shadows of running dogs.

King signaled the team to move.

"I was just thinking," Duke said, "my sniper rifle's deadweight in this darkness. The scope gathers light, but there needs to be *some* ambient illumination for me to even pick up a target. It's getting pitch-black out here."

Hoffman knew the sniper was correct. The situation was bad and their equipment worse. They were rushing into failure and no amount of *elan* would make up for a bad plan.

The supply depot was an enormous warehouse surrounded by a large parking lot and access roads. A simple fence lined the outer perimeter and Steuben vaulted it easily, landing on the other side in a crouch with his rifle ready.

Garrison and King attempted the fence next, making too much noise and taking far too long to negotiate the obstacle. King hit the ground first, tucking and rolling into a shooting position. Garrison got his hand caught near the top and dangled for a second before dropping awkwardly to his feet, grunting as air was knocked from his lungs.

"I bet Opal does better than that," Max said.

"Up and over, hotshot," Booker said to Max.

"Enough chatter; just get it done," King snapped.

Hoffman did his best not to embarrass himself. He heard his team complaining about the lack of power armor that would make the maneuver easier and appreciated King's exhortations for them to deal with it. They moved across the open area to the first building.

King took half the team around the perimeter of the building and support buildings. Hoffman followed Garrison and Steuben, keeping Opal with him.

"LT, we have contact with the personnel here. I think they crapped themselves when they saw Steuben, but I calmed them down. The local chief wants to talk to who's in charge," Garrison said. "Which is you."

Chapter 11

Hoffman ran forward to control the situation and found a sturdily built foreman looking pale and jittery.

"Lieutenant Thomas Hoffman, Strike Marines. Do you have injured?"

The civilian supply chief held a shotgun uncomfortably and shifted his weight foot to foot. Looking uncomfortable around an officer, he gave a lopsided quasi salute. "No one got hurt, sir. I didn't see the Beast, but Jake over there said he did. We went inside and locked the doors. Didn't expect it with the sun not all the way down yet."

"How long has it been since you sighted it?"

The man wiped sweat from his forehead. "'Bout thirty minutes. Keep hearing it. Are you gonna blast it?"

King jogged over to Hoffman. "It's going to take some getting used to, not being able to just call you. Anyhow, we're basically set up. I did a run around the perimeter. Most of the civilians have been evacuated or locked inside. The supply depot is basically a warehouse with too many access points for good security."

"Recommendations?" Hoffman asked.

"I don't know where else to put the civilians, so we'll leave that to local security forces. For now, make sure they're bunkered down. Set up strong points and wait. Try to get a good look at this thing." King paused and gathered his thoughts before adding, "I'm not interested in chasing shadows that might kill us without at least knowing what this thing is. I mean, how big is it? What are its methods of attack? Is there more than one?"

"I agree," Hoffman said. "Pass it along to the team."

Steuben grunted. "It is good working with Strike Marines again. Even if they can't climb the fence without high-tech armor."

Hoffman put Duke and Booker on the northeast corner with binoculars and Duke's high-powered sniper scope. He placed King and Gor'al on the southeast corner, Max and Steuben on the southwest, and took the northwest with Opal.

The night passed slowly, long stretches of boredom punctuated by parachute flares and alarms. It was excruciatingly quiet once the monster switched from harassing them to stalking them. He couldn't get on the radio for updates and Opal wasn't much of a conversationalist.

"Every five or ten minutes, Opie. I think it's playing with us," Hoffman muttered as a tangle of tin cans was dragged across an alleyway just out of view.

"Opal doesn't like that noise."

"Me neither. It's an effective alarm mechanism, but crude. Wonder whose kids are missing their treehouse alarms."

The cans clattered in the darkness. Around a nearby building, firecrackers went off, the snap too weak to be mistaken for gunshots.

Hoffman considered shouting to King but disregarded the idea when he imagined them yelling updates back and forth until morning. "Opal, should we use the radio? I think we can risk it. Maybe draw it into the open."

"Opal no use radio. Opal just stay here and look for enemy."

"Right. Stick to the plan. Maybe I should promote you."

"Opal work. Opal no officer."

Hoffman chuckled as quietly as he could as another

flare launched into the air and drifted lazily.

"Contact!" Max shouted, and he fired a three-round burst through a busted window. "Big and mean-looking! Moving fast and coming right for us, LT! I say again, the Beast is circling our perimeter. Running between buildings and power conduits."

Hoffman braced himself against the wall. He expected to hear it before he saw it but was disappointed. One moment his ears were ringing from Max's machine-gun blasts, the next he heard a crash from across the small parking lot.

Hoffman swung his muzzle up to a nearby window just as an illumination shell burst in the sky.

The shifting light of the flare dangling by a parachute swept over the open space and a pair of red eyes gleamed from a misplaced shadow. The Beast was matte-black, its body long and sleek with an exoskeleton at odd angles, no symmetry anywhere but the elongated triangle of its head. Multiple tails thrashed with sparks as it crouched back on its hind legs and leapt toward Hoffman's building in a blur of legs.

Hoffman aimed and fired a single shot, the recoil knocking him back a step and sending a sharp pain through his shoulder. He was so used to fighting in power armor that the simpler weapon had taken him by surprise.

Opal had no such problems and used his bulk to steady his weapon as he emptied a magazine in quick order.

Sparks flew off the Beast as more rounds from the Marines hit home. It turned sharply and vanished down an alleyway.

"Opal, did you hit it?"

"Yes, sir. Opal 6-1-9 struck the creature three times on its leg, twice on the torso, and once on its head."

"Good shooting, Opie." He pivoted from his position and shouted, "It's coming around! We scored definite hits."

"On it," Duke called out from the roof, then gave an uncharacteristic whoop. "Let me show you how it's done!"

Several rounds of controlled gunfire erupted from Duke and Booker's position.

"Give me an update," Hoffman shouted. By the time Duke and Booker answered, Garrison and Gor'al were spraying the target with rifle bursts.

"I don't know if you hit it, but it's moving a lot faster than it was," Garrison shouted. "Maybe we wounded it, but I think we just pissed it off. You'd think these damn elephant guns would slow it down."

Hoffman saw the Beast twice more, but from a distance and only silhouetted against lamplight.

"Stay ready," he shouted over the growing ringing in his ears. Hearing damage from the gunfire was another thing he'd forgotten to plan for—forgotten it would get increasingly difficult to alert someone the Beast was coming right for them because they couldn't hear the warning.

"LT, we saw it head north," Duke called out. "We going after it?"

Hoffman hesitated long enough to vigorously rub the back of his neck.

"Opal needs more bullets."

"You need a bigger weapon, Opie." Hoffman tossed a magazine to the doughboy then shouted to Duke, "Let's go! Let us catch up and form a QRF to handle it when it turns to fight. If you outpace us, abort the track and rally back here. King, let's get the team moving."

"Yes, sir," King replied. "You heard the man. Bring it in."

A minute later, his team was in the parking lot, crouched around a lorry.

"No signal flares from anywhere else," Hoffman said. "It must have doubled back the way it came. We make and maintain contact and destroy the Beast. Look sharp. A lot of Pathfinders and Marines have already died trying to take this thing down."

"It's one step ahead of us. Keeps turning corners." Booker was winded but enthusiastic after taking several flights of stairs.

"King, watch our six," Hoffman said.

"Absolutely, LT."

"We may have something," Booker said, glancing down at a printed map. "It's about to cross a drainage canal that one of the locals said is mostly empty—just a trickle of water running down the center. This will be the only time we have the high ground. The angle's funny and the range is a stretch, but it's the best chance we're going to get for a decent shot with the sniper rifle."

"I need to be higher," Duke said.

Hoffman raced forward with the team. "Duke, take Opal in case he needs to hoist you onto something."

"Opal throw Duke."

"Settle down, big guy. I'll say when I need a boost. Don't want you pitching me to the moon," Duke drawled.

"Opal boost Duke."

The sniper shook his head. "Come on, then. Stay low and be quiet."

Hoffman watched them run off and then said to the rest of the team, "Garrison and Booker, King and Gor'al, Steuben and Max with me in the center. Let's advance in a wedge on me and stay out of sight. We may need to swing a flank around quickly if we get this thing pinned."

Steuben frowned. "We should advance in a line. Unimaginative but quicker to envelop the Beast when we catch it."

"You're the hunter here, Steuben," Hoffman said. "What's it doing?"

"It's acting wrong," the Karigole said. "Predators do not expose themselves before they attack. It used itself to draw fire, test our numbers."

"I'm with you on that, Steuben. It's been probing positions all night. Why?" King asked.

"To know where to strike," Steuben said. "Being mobile and aggressive will throw it off. We're doing the right thing."

"A bunker would be mighty nice right about now," Max said. "I feel like a mobile buffet for that thing."

"I'm going up to the power relay, which is shut off due to current events." Duke slapped Booker on the shoulder and the two peeled off.

Hoffman came to a bridge that overlooked the drainage area. "Team, get in line."

"Garrison and I have something," Booker shouted from a few meters to Hoffman's left. "Fast-moving shadow ascending the other side of the concrete spillway. Range three hundred meters."

"Duke?" Hoffman touched his ear, reaching for an IR transmitter that wasn't there. "Blast it, we need mirrors for signaling, something."

"I've got a running list of best practices we're missing," King said. "Long list."

The sharp crack of Duke's rifle broke through the air and Hoffman glanced over the guardrails and saw the Beast just inside the drainage tunnel.

"Light it up!" Hoffman yelled as he opened fire. A heartbeat later, the rest of his team joined in, leaning on the railing of the bridge and emptying their magazines.

The Beast vanished back into the tunnel.

"I don't know about you, but I drilled whatever that was several times," King said. "Looked like a big cat, but weird, like it was made up of polygons or something."

"Where is it?" Hoffman asked as King and the others shifted positions.

"I'm not seeing it," Garrison said. "But if we're not hurting it with these slugs, we might as well switch to spitballs and harsh language."

"It's gone," Max said.

Hoffman looked at Steuben.

The Karigole growled. "It got away. Again. I am starting to agree with the complainer. We need bigger weapons. And we need to be ready for an attack. If its pattern holds, the moment we lose sight of it, it will begin hunting us."

"Which is getting to be a familiar pattern," Max said.

"Form up and move out," Hoffman said. "Sniper team will stay on overwatch. Rest of us will cross the bridge in two teams, bounding overwatch. King, lead off."

King, Gor'al, Garrison, and Max moved forward, two on each side of the bridge providing cross cover for each other. Hoffman, Steuben, and Opal's section covered the long angles, aiming into shadows over iron sights, waiting for a glimpse of the Beast. Duke and Booker remained in their sniper perch on overwatch.

King and his team reached the far end of the bridge and signaled Hoffman.

"Let's go. Look sharp."

Sweat ran down Hoffman's back. His team was in prime physical condition, but they were used to their power armor taking the slack off what they carried and keeping their body temperature regulated. They were more than ready for the dressed-down requirements of this mission, but it didn't make the event fun. It was disturbingly solitary beneath his helmet. He'd never realized how much radio chatter his team indulged in until it was taken away.

"Steuben and Opal, move up," Hoffman said before going to King and kneeling beside him. "We'll move into the next section of the city and search for it. Go slow. I don't want to rush to failure. Gathering intelligence is nearly as important as taking the thing down. Hopefully, these cameras are taking decent pictures."

"Understood." King signaled his squad and led the

way. Before long, both squads were clearing street to street, moving silently under the stars of Eridu. No one lit candles or lamps in this part of the city and the flares fell less frequently.

"We're coming up. I don't want to be too dispersed here," Hoffman said as his team crept along the wall of a partially collapsed building to join King and the others.

"Looks like a ship went down here," Max said. "How many did the locals lose before they learned not to fly over the city?"

"A lot in this neighborhood. It must be in the flight path to the airport," Hoffman said.

"Wait," Steuben said. "I hear it."

Hoffman's blood ran cold.

The Karigole shifted foot to foot, flaring his nostrils as he turned his face upward and toward the wall. He whispered, which made him sound particularly ominous. "It's on the other side of this wall…but I can't smell it."

Max pulled a frag grenade from his tactical vest.

Hoffman put a hand on his to stop him, shaking his head minutely. The wall wasn't thick and the blast would punch right through it and the Marines. Max went pale as the same realization hit him and he carefully locked the grenade back onto his vest.

Hoffman looked around. Steuben was gone.

The sound of gentle clinks and a rustle of something big against the other side of wall sent a chill down Hoffman's spine, a chill he refused to acknowledge as fear.

Hoffman tapped King on the shoulder then jerked a thumb over his shoulder to where Steuben should have been. King did a double take, then shrugged.

Shuffling back from the wall, Hoffman leveled his weapon at it and slapped fingers against the muzzle twice to get the rest of the team's attention. They passed a bump down the line until the signal reached the Dotari.

Gor'al turned slightly, bumping his helmet camera

against the wall. His camera sprang into action, taking a burst of photographs.

Hoffman clenched at the noise, wincing internally as he counted each second with a heartbeat that pounded like a bass drum.

A second passed, then another.

The Beast punched through the wall, claws of three arms slashing toward Gor'al.

Hoffman retreated a step and opened fire through concrete and plaster. Fragments exploded around each bullet strike. Some went through. Others ricocheted.

The Beast's claws wrapped around Gor'al's helmet. Ripping his own claw through the chin strap, Gor'al ducked away, firing blind at the Beast.

"Do you think I can miss from this distance? I'll kill you and your bovine leavings!"

"Gor'al, no!" Hoffman shifted position to get a better firing angle. Booker and the others couldn't get a shot without hitting the Dotari Marine.

The thing on the other side of the wall roared. A second later, the wall exploded outward. Gor'al flew backward, arms and legs akimbo as he struck the pavement in the middle of the street. King was tumbled sideways and Garrison and Max were lost in an avalanche of shattered wall fragments and dust.

Hoffman dropped and rolled to one side, coming clumsily to his feet. The balance of his ballistic gear was different from his Strike Marine armor. His awareness of the encumbrance was a fleeting thought, background noise in his mind. His eyes focused on his target, shuffling the sensory overload as his finger squeezed the trigger. The weapon barked, recoiling with surprising force.

Moving, shooting, searching for a clear angle on the target took all his attention. Opal and the others were in the fight now, ripping off rounds while he reloaded.

Mortar flares swung down from the sky, more and

more of them as the fight continued. Somewhere, an alert guard was trying to help. The inconsistent light reflected from the dust thrown into the air by the conflict. Muzzle flashes of the low-tech assault rifles turned the scene into a disco ball in hell.

"Where the hell is Steuben?" King yelled.

Hoffman didn't answer. Instead, he lunged forward and grabbed Gor'al by the back of his armor and pulled him out of the maelstrom.

The Beast lashed out from the cloud of dust and ripped claws across Hoffman's chest. A talon hooked in the flack vest, sending Hoffman flying to one side and into the remnants of the wall, helmet-first.

Opal roared and dropped his rifle. The doughboy swung his war hammer off his shoulder blindly into the dust. There was a clang of the hammer hitting home and Opal stumbled back, the weapon shaking loose from his grip and bouncing in the rubble, vibrating wildly.

Something crossed Hoffman's vision and a fire erupted in the smoke. The Beast reared up on its hind legs, its fire-coated arms spread wide like a demon emerging from hell. The thing twisted around and loped away, trailing flame.

Holding a bottle with a lit wick in one hand, Steuben put the other on Hoffman's chest. The lieutenant looked down at the three deep gouges that had penetrated his vest, exposing his flesh. Thin lines of blood glittered in the light from the Karigole's firebomb.

"You're barely even bleeding," Steuben said.

"It hurts, if that matters." Hoffman winced and found his rifle in the rubble.

The Beast tore down a road to an open rent in the city's outer fence. The crack of Duke's sniper rifle carried through the air, but if the shots connected, they didn't have any obvious effect on the creature as it vanished into the jungle.

Steuben snuffed out the wick, a lit bit of cloth, with his bare hand.

"Where the hell were you?" Hoffman asked.

"Don't you know how to fight from the shadows?" Steuben asked. He touched his artificial eye and turned it back on. "I watched it follow your heat traces across the ground after our first fight with it. I realized it must see in the infrared spectrum—from its second set of eyes, perhaps. There wasn't an opportunity to make a firebomb before now."

Hoffman stared at him, dumbstruck.

"We had to get close enough, and I needed something to improvise into an explosive device. As soon as we heard it on the other side of the wall, I went back to one of the shops we passed. I have been making a mental note of where there are lamps and other incendiary devices all night."

"Why didn't you say something earlier? We're part

of a team, remember?"

"It was a dynamic situation. I saw an opportunity and took it. If I had said something, the Beast would have attacked sooner."

"I could have made you a real bomb," Garrison said. "It's what I do. You want one that just burns, I can do that. You want one that knocks down a wall, I'm your guy. Didn't they have breachers and explosives experts when you fought with Strike Marines?"

Steuben glared at Garrison. "Perhaps you can finally prove useful."

"Most people want to stay on the bomb guy's good side," Garrison said as he let his rifle hang loose at his waist. "Did we…win? We managed to drive it off."

"It'll be back." Max knelt in the rubble and picked up a shard of obsidian. "Look, this must be part of it's—ow!" He dropped the shard and shook his hand. The shard went red-hot and disintegrated.

"Explains why the locals have never found a trace of it," King said. "That remind you of anything, Lieutenant?"

"Xaros drones disintegrate when destroyed." Hoffman worked his boot in the dust where the fragment had vanished. "But not like that. No heat."

"Please tell me we didn't find the *other* last Xaros drone in the galaxy," Garrison said.

"We what?" Steuben asked.

"That's not what we're dealing with," Hoffman said. "I saw the drone on the *Kidran's Gift* up close and personal. This isn't the same thing. There's nothing…primal…about the Xaros."

"At least we've got that going for us," Max said.

"We know it sees on the infrared spectrum and that fire is a useful tool." Hoffman tapped the camera on the side of his helmet. "Anyone get footage?"

Garrison took his helmet off and flipped a switch on

the camera.

"It's on now," he muttered.

Gor'al picked up his half-crushed helmet from the rubble and picked through long threads of exposed film.

"Perhaps we can salvage something from this?" the Dotari asked and then chattered in his native tongue as he walked in a circle, fidgeting with the wrecked camera.

"We need Booker to check out Gor," Hoffman said, waving a hand toward the sniper perch.

"Thing work?" Opal thrust his helmet into Hoffman's chest, which sent sharp pain through his scratches. The camera on the doughboy's helmet ticked, out of film.

"Let's get it back to the lab and see what develops," Hoffman said, dabbing his fingertips at the cuts on his chest.

"You got lucky, sir," King said.

"Don't I know it. Stay tactical. The Beast might

come back for round two."

****

Every muscle in Hoffman's body ached. His team moved like they'd been in a tough fight, their aches and pains evident. They slept whenever and wherever they could, and Garrison, Booker, and King were out cold near the door to the lab. Heads propped up on helmets and feet crossed, they held their weapons across their bodies as they snored. Opal stood over them, eyes half closed.

Hoffman sat in a chair as Masako dabbed the cuts in his chest with a swab.

"That's what I should be doing," Max said absently as he watched Lilith Yarrow remove the film from the developer canister. "I had an uncle who used to do antique photography. Soaked the stuff in fluid and then hung it up to dry. Never really understood it. I was just a kid."

"He was probably soaking it in distilled water to swell the gelatin layer," Lilith said. "This method is a series of baths. Very straightforward. I get in a kind of meditative state by the end of it."

"I could see that. Very cool tech. So retro."

"The most important thing is the non-ionic rinse," she said.

Masako put the bloody swab into a box and a screen lit up. "Not the way I would have retrieved a gene sample," she said. "I admire your dedication. Feeling well? Fever? Double vision? Sensation of an alien presence gestating in your thoracic cavity?"

"What was that last part?" Hoffman asked.

Masako held a palm over Hoffman's chest and a light glowed out from a sensor glove. "Nothing. You're good." She glanced down at the box and frowned. "No presence of any alien DNA in the wound at all…you sure the Beast did this?"

"There any other giant black creatures attacking the city?" the lieutenant asked.

"You're done with him," Booker said, tapping Masako on the shoulder. "He's mine to patch up."

"Bit disappointing…" Masako's braced arm gave Hoffman a gentle pat on the shoulder. "Not you. That there's nothing to examine, other than the claw marks, I mean. Someone's calling me." She hurried away and Booker took her place in front of the bare-chested Hoffman.

"You won't even have a scar after I fix you up," Booker said.

Hoffman massaged his face to wake up, doing his best to ignore the medic as she ran a flesh knitter over his cuts.

Max came over, flapping pictures. "Got something," he said. "We all saw it up close and personal. Now everyone else can too."

He passed Hoffman a photo, but Steuben snatched it out of his hand, held the picture up to the light, and then muttered something in Karigole that Hoffman took as a curse. Max handed the lieutenant another picture.

It was a snap of the Beast's triangular head against a flare descending through the sky. Small ridges ran down the angles, while a single bale-red eye stared without any evident emotion.

"It is like nothing I've seen," Steuben said. "No match for any predator on this planet. For as many times as we hit it, no one found a single blood trail."

"If it can't bleed," Garrison said with a yawn and a stretch, "can we kill it?"

"Xaros don't bleed." Steuben tapped a knuckle of his mechanical hand against his prosthetic eye. "And I've seen them die."

"I feel better," Garrison said.

"That's sarcasm." Gor'al held up a finger. "Sarcasm

detected, yes?"

Booker and Duke patted the Dotari Marine on his shoulders and he rustled his quills, pleased with the close proximity and praise.

Garrison leaned closer to take in the pictures. "Man, that thing is horrifying."

"I think we found our official team photographer," Booker said. "Good job, Opal. At least you remembered to turn your equipment on. Gor'al's film got ruined by direct exposure after his camera was smashed."

Opal opened one eye, then went back to rest mode.

"He's got my vote, if he can keep his smash-it-until-it-doesn't-move programming in check. One unstoppable killing machine smashes through a wall and Gor pisses himself," Duke said. "I wish I had video of that."

Hoffman rubbed his temples. "Our rifles didn't even tickle the damn thing. I can't see that the fire did much except confuse it. We need our gauss rifles and anti-tank grenades."

Lilith shook her head. "That's not an option. The moment you activate those weapons, it will be all over you. The power signature generated by a gauss weapon has the most acute effect on the Beast of anything we've seen. We lost three teams before we figured that out."

Colonel Fallon and Yarrow arrived. They spoke quietly with Lilith for a moment as she showed them the developed photos.

"Permission to speak freely, Colonel?" Duke asked.

"Granted."

"The Beast zeros in and wrecks any artificial power source it detects. We get it. But in my expert opinion, we need to put it in a box and hit it with something that will actually damage it. We're wasting our time with these peashooters. Don't get me wrong—I want to keep mine when we're done, but even my sniper rifle is useless for this mission."

King paced forward, glaring at the pictures as he spoke. "We can carry gauss weapons without the batteries plugged in. Bring them online when it's time to shoot. There's a forty-five-second charge time…during which we'll be vulnerable. Sucks, but it's our only option. Am I wrong, Steuben?"

"We know what attracts the creature. We know what to use as bait."

"Is he going to say me? I think he means me," Garrison said. "Stop looking at me like that."

"Don't you want to make something go boom?" Duke asked the breacher.

"What kind of question is that?"

"I brought you all to Eridu for solutions," Fallon said. "Let's hear it."

"We tracked it to the edge of the city after lighting it on fire," Hoffman said.

Steuben stepped forward. "We must track it down

in the jungle. Its lair is the underground lab with the Qa'Resh artifacts, yes? The jungle will prove a better hunting ground. Fewer risks to civilians in the city and we will have more room to chase it down. Everything needs to eat and rest. The daylight hours are our best chance to lay a trap."

"Sleep is overrated," Max muttered.

"If it's sleeping in the lab," Hoffman said, "why don't we call in a kinetic strike from the *Scipio*? End this the easy way."

"And destroy the artifacts?" Fallon shook his head. "We don't know for sure the lab is the Beast's bed-down location. Union High Command was explicit that the artifacts are mission critical."

"But our lives aren't?" Gor'al asked.

"Mission first, people always." Fallon's face darkened. "I don't like it either. How can anything be that valuable—ancient civilization or not?"

"I witnessed a Qa'Resh planetary defense laser used against the Xaros," Steuben said. "It wiped out millions of drones as easily as you could flip a light switch. The ancients' technology can and will upset the balance of power in the galaxy."

"No wonder the Ibarras want it all so badly," Hoffman said, glancing down at three thin pink strips of skin across his chest.

"But orbital artillery is an option," Fallon said. "Spot the Beast away from the lab and signal the target location to the *Scipio*. Kinetic strikes don't require guidance systems. Let gravity do all the work. Swamps absorb a lot of the kinetic force from an artillery bombardment. We'll make a big mess, but not necessarily damage the lab. So you'll have to put eyes on it and make a determination of which is the best course."

Hoffman nodded. "Agreed. I doubt we'll find it asleep in its lair. That's where the real plan will kick in."

Steuben growled a word Hoffman didn't know.

"The advantage of the swamp is we can hide our heat signatures. The city is an artificial environment, easy to see things on the infrared spectrum."

"Especially if you're a face-eating alien construct designed to fight off Xaros drones," Garrison said.

"We need to move quickly and scout the terrain. When it starts to hunt, we draw it into a kill zone and Duke takes it out with his rail rifle," Steuben said. "If we can chip away at it with our assault rifles, then his weapon—"

"Give me a clear shot with Ice Claw and I'll turn that thing into dust," the sniper said.

"High-powered shots from gauss rifles could manage to disable it," King said. "Then Garrison can chime in."

"Ain't no problem in this galaxy that high explosives can't solve," the breacher said.

"You power up gauss tech, you'll be in a world of

hurt," Fallon said.

"Sitting around won't kill the Beast," Hoffman said. "Better to take a risk and succeed than wait for inevitable failure. There's a war against the Kesaht we all want to get back to."

Long, uncomfortable moments passed.

Fallon was the highest-ranking military authority on the planet and Hoffman respected him.

Rubbing his chin with a hand that held his chopped-down cigar, Fallon said, "There's a lot of things that can go wrong. I expect the execution of the plan will look nothing like the planning of the plan. We all know the maxim about first contact. Do it."

"Oorah," Hoffman said evenly.

"Get with the quartermaster and draw the gear you need," Fallon said.

Duke rubbed his hands together quickly and smiled.

Chapter 12

Masha strode down the hallway, smoothing her lab coat nervously—a ridiculous emotion. Seventeen alien worlds in twelve standard months—and nearly as many missions—and she was afraid of being called out about a simple forgery? Eleven forgeries, actually, but who was counting?

"I have nothing to worry about," she muttered, feeling for the nearly invisible dart packet she kept under the cuff of her jacket. "There's always plan B. Or plan C. Or random-ass improvisation."

She checked her reflection in one of the monitor screens, happy with her hair and understated makeup. The glasses she didn't need were a nice touch, but probably the source of her nervousness—taking a disguise too far could be a weakness.

Unable to delay, she swiped her identification card and entered the laboratory. Her glasses were fine. What were the chances a building full of the smartest people on the planet would notice they were fake?

She calmed her breathing and cleared her mind. "You called for me, Mrs. Yarrow?"

Lilith Yarrow, not an unattractive woman, crossed her arms and stared. A bit taller than Masha, she wore the same style of lab coat, and although she lacked any rank insignia or other obvious markings of authority, her presence was intimidating.

Fragments of ancient technology were spread across three tables. Protractors, slide rulers, and notes taken on actual graph paper supplemented modern scanners, electron microscopes, and infrared spectroscopy stations. Frequent limitations on the use of electronic devices inspired creativity she'd never expected from these science types.

Masha swiped back a strand of hair, checking for exits.

"The Qa'resh tech you delivered are fakes. An explanation is required," Lilith said, pointing a metal stylus grounded against electricity at what could have been the skin of a metal apple. Missing circuits left gaps around the top hemisphere of the device. Scorch marks seemed to have originated from the core of the item. "We know this is an insulation sphere…not something that ever had internal power. The scorching should have been limited to the outside of the device."

"I don't understand," Masha said, pretending to study the device.

"It's a fake."

"How can that be? They came from Pathfinders on the northern galactic rim. They've always been my most trusted sources of archaeotech."

Lilith shifted her stance but didn't uncross her arms or look away. "What tests did you use to verify authenticity? Did your sources find these items themselves or pick them up from somebody else? I normally trust the Pathfinders, but they're not scientists."

Masha made a show of touring the worktables with barely suppressed anxiety. A staff-like object with four prongs at the end was real—mixed in with the fakes to lend credibility. She knew which pieces were real because she had collected the items herself from lost worlds—the most recent from Koen. Other pieces…they were probably fake. She bought them to help bolster her cover as an expert in the field of Qa'Resh archeology. It'd been a calculated risk.

Lilith stepped to a table insulated against electrical currents and picked up a scythe-shaped book with dead screens instead of pages. "This piece has been sorely mishandled over the years. I'm finding residue of multiple worlds on it, which means it's probably been bouncing around in somebody's cargo hold for years until he or she realized it was valuable. Whoever brought this to you bought it off the black market."

Despite her complete lack of emotion, Masha made her face turn red with anger, a skill she'd learned early in her spy training. People were easy to fool when they expected a person to act a certain way. The nervousness had passed. She was in her element now.

"Are you saying I cut corners? I assure you, I was meticulous in my review of these items. I'm certain these are not fakes. Just where do you get off questioning my expertise?" Masha asked, holding her gaze firm, her nose slightly raised to elicit just the right response.

"You're new here." Lilith slammed the fake against the table. "So very new, so I'll cut you just a little bit of slack. Akkadians—of which I'm one, in case you missed which planet you're on—have worked with Qa'resh technology for hundreds—yes, hundreds—of years. The Toth imprisoned my ancestors, tricked them into believing they were gods, not monsters, and we hacked a Qa'Resh probe, and bent it to the Toth's will. *I* was the senior scientist under the Toth until my husband and the *Breitenfeld* saved us."

Yes, keep talking, Masha thought as she looked down at her feet, feigning embarrassment.

"Eridu has been the Terran Union's main lab studying Qa'Resh tech since Marc and Stacey Ibarra went rogue, and I am *still* the top scientist. So if I tell you something is a fake, it is a Saint-damned fake, you understand me?"

"Yes, Dr. Yarrow." Masha fought back a smile. Mighty kind of Lilith to identify herself as the primary target of Masha's mission to Eridu. Her knowledge would serve Lady Ibarra's needs…just how to get her back to Navarre was a different problem.

Three beeps sounded from the public-address system. "All personnel, stand by for scheduled power-down. This is a security measure. All personnel, stand by for scheduled power-down."

Lilith frowned and turned her back on Masha, walking briskly to a computer station to type vigorously. Data entry complete, she just as abruptly moved to the next table. "These three devices are most assuredly fakes. This one has potential. It may not be Qa'Resh, but they may have used it."

"Expensive, but probably worth it. Fakes have long been the bane of archeologists," Lilith said. "I apologize if I alarmed you. Confrontation isn't really my thing."

Masha feigned humility. "Have I thanked you for the opportunity to work on Eridu? It's the center of science and discovery right now. If not for the local dangers and the war, this planet would be the new Oxford, or Harvard or—"

Lilith rolled her eyes.

Masha moved closer, then placed one hand on Lilith's shoulder. A second passed, and she knew she'd slipped past an important trust barrier. "You seem stressed. I'm sorry if I'm the cause."

Lilith stepped away, closing a tablet she'd been using to take notes. "It's not you, or the work, or that damn Beast. I have a child off world—well, not so childish now, but she'll always be my baby. Sorry, I'm being one of those parents who annoy nonparents. It's not your problem."

Masha hugged herself. "I'm from a big family. Mother and Father argued a lot, usually about our well-being. I'm sorry about all this. Costs of the career, right?"

"Something like that," Lilith said.

"So what did I do wrong? I'd like to avoid paying for a fake in the future. If my grant money comes through, I'll have a team to excavate more of the archaeotech myself. But I still have to contract the really dangerous stuff…like you suggested."

Lilith paused. "That's a good way to react. I'm sorry if I insulted you earlier. The fakes aren't your fault. I've just never seen that many forgeries at once. It's weird."

Well, we had to see which of you Akkadians were smart enough to pick them out, Masha thought. *And you didn't disappoint.*

"Where's your library?" Masha asked. "I need to study your research. You must have so much that can be put to use by the right people."

****

Masha stretched her arms up, noting the reflection of an armed guard passing by the lab.

"My coffee's cold. Would you mind if I took a break?" Masha asked Lilith.

"Go ahead," Lilith said without looking up from her microscope.

"Want anything?"

Lilith didn't answer.

Masha stepped into the hallway, found a drinking fountain, and dumped the untouched coffee. No one was around. She tapped her ear once to activate the quantum dot device in her ear.

"Medvedev, are you there?"

"I am. On a work detail to the western bunkers, filling in sand bags."

"You sound jealous I'm in air-conditioning. You legionnaires too good for manual labor?"

"My cover demands this. Hard work for the body is good work for the soul. What do you need?"

She went to the corner and glanced around it to be sure no one was eavesdropping on her. She'd picked this hallway because the cameras were poorly positioned and easy to evade. "I've identified a target, Lilith Yarrow, an expert on Qa'Resh tech. She saw through the fakes immediately. The others believed everything I gave them was real. Imbeciles."

"You serve the Lady well…when you're not captured." Medvedev sounded half asleep.

"Such an ass, my little bear. You were just as captured as I was that last time, remember?" Something tickled Masha's spine, so she walked toward the lounge to "refill" her coffee as Lilith Yarrow's husband came around the next corner. This Yarrow, the former Strike Marine medic-turned-doctor, talked with his hands, his enthusiasm evident as he spoke of the research facility.

Masha caught herself as she saw the Karigole behind Yarrow, but her heart skipped a beat when she caught a glimpse of Hoffman with the big alien.

Ducking into the break room and opening a refrigerator, the spy bent over, blocking her face from the doorway as Yarrow and the others went by. Masha kept her head in the room-temperature fridge, smelling lunches that had succumbed to the power outage.

She reached into her lab coat and gripped the small pistol loaded with dumdum bullets, but getting made and shooting her way out of this building was not her mission. She wondered just how many times she'd have to hit the Karigole.

"Problem," Masha said.

"Elaborate."

"That Union dog Hoffman is here. In my work area." Masha ran a hand through her hair, wishing she'd dyed it to cover the distinctive platinum-blonde strands before she arrived on Eridu.

"Is he looking for you?"

Masha peeked over the refrigerator door and saw Yarrow's tour turn into the lab where Lilith worked.

"Doubt it. He'd be armed and have the rest of his

mutts with him. Do you think that doughboy is finally dead? Probably not…" She repeated an expletive over and over again, trying to remember her exit plan for the building.

"*Can you eliminate Hoffman?*" Medvedev asked.

"Not the mission," Masha said.

"Excuse me," came from the doorway.

Reaching into her coat, Masha gripped the pistol, turned slowly, and found Yarrow blocking her only way out.

"It's Martha, right?" Yarrow asked.

"Yes, sir." Masha gave him her best smile.

"The other Doctor Yarrow needs you to go to tube room four and pick up a transfer from the university. I'm here for coffee. There extra cups?"

"Top shelf. We're out of creamer. Excuse me." Her heart racing, Masha slipped past him and went down the hallway with as much speed as she could muster without drawing attention.

She slipped into the tube room and put her back to the door, pneumatic tubes clunking and hissing as canisters shot through them. A stack of tubes the width of plumbing lines rattled as a plastic cylinder rattled into a basket.

On the bottom level was a much larger tube—wide enough that Masha could crawl inside.

"Medvedev…" She rapped knuckles against the big tube. "Where do these big lines run?"

"All through the city. We had shovels delivered to our work area that way. It is rather efficient."

"I have an idea."

"Very nice, Doctor," Hoffman's voice carried through the door. Masha drew her pistol and went to one knee, training the muzzle on the door. "But it doesn't help us with the Beast…" The Strike Marine's conversation faded as he went down the hallway.

Masha let out a sigh and re-holstered her weapon

just as the door burst open and Lilith put a hand to her hip.

"There a problem?" she asked.

"Just…" Masha began, picking up a stray piece of paper, "dropped something. Sorry, ma'am. Your sample's here." She picked out the canister and handed it over.

"You missed a war hero," Lilith said. "Steuben the Karigole. You ever see that *Last Stand on Takeni* movie?"

"Hasn't everyone?"

"Don't mention it to Steuben if you do run into him. He'll bite your face off."

"Sounds like my kind of person," Medvedev said.

Masha ran her hand over her ear and shut off the transmitter.

Chapter 13

As his team moved slowly through the early morning jungle, Hoffman pulled his leg from the muck, nearly losing his boot, which would've been unthinkable in his regular gear. Sabatons integrated into modern Strike Marine armor and stayed on unless there was an explosive amputation. On Eridu, no amount of fatigue blousing and one-hundred-mile-an-hour tape could keep the ooze from his socks, which meant he couldn't tie his boots tight enough to guarantee the continued benefits of footwear.

"Whose idea was this?" Garrison complained from the front. "And why am I always on point? Do you want me to get eaten?"

"Opal not let Garrison get eaten," said the doughboy, who sank to his mid-thighs while the breacher was up to his waist in murky water.

A cloud of mosquitoes rose up from the bogs around them and advanced like a swarm of tiny Xaros drones. Hoffman checked his gear to be sure there weren't any openings. "I'll be glad to get back to regular armor just to keep the bugs out."

"You see? That's what I'm talking about," Garrison said. "Every single planet has little biters that love the way I taste. Oh, good. More rain."

Sheets of precipitation fell straight down, pounding Hoffman's helmet until he could barely hear himself think, and visibility dropped to nothing. He thought the mosquitoes would retreat, but they didn't. "Someone check on Gor'al."

"I've got him," Booker said.

"None of you believe me that I've never been in a swamp before. How was I to know about quicksand?" the Dotari asked.

"You know about quicksand by looking at quicksand. What made you think you could wade through it?" Booker asked.

"I'm walking through this. What could be the difference? The quicksand looked more solid than this *tharji* piss pretending to be water."

Exercising the first lesson in officer candidate school, Hoffman climbed onto a rotting tree stump and counted his people. The days of glancing into his HUD to check their status were behind him for the foreseeable future. Exercising the second lesson, situational awareness, he asked, "King, anything following us?"

"Negative. Not yet," King replied as something wet worked its way up Hoffman's pants leg. He smacked it hard, thinking it could be a snake. Duke and Max looked at him.

"False alarm. Thought I had a visitor."

Duke lifted his visor to spit chewing tobacco into the swamp. "Good to know. I made the mistake of looking up if there's a local variant of candiru fish or piranhas."

"Well?" Garrison looked over his shoulder. "Are there?"

"You'll know when you feel something nibble on your pecker hole," Duke said.

"You all talk too much," grumbled Steuben, who seemed more at home in the swamp than anyone else. "Reminds me of Standish. I wish Gunney Cortaro had followed up on his many promises to that yammering little puppy."

"I have a few ideas about what Cortaro had in mind," King said.

As the rain abated, a pair of drones shot overhead. On a normal day, Hoffman would've been glad to see them, since the devices provided real-time intelligence in battle and boosted his confidence. These made him feel vulnerable. The IR transmitter in his ear gave him updates and linked him to Fallon and Yarrow in the city while taunting the Beast to come out of its lair.

One by one, his team looked up as the drones weaved among trees and hanging vines.

"You're making me nervous with those things, LT," Booker said.

Gor'al nodded vigorously. "Me as well. How do they not ruin our plan?"

"Don't worry, the drones will go down before the Beast shows up to eat our guts." Hoffman wished he felt as confident as he sounded. Their plan relied on drawing the Beast at a specific time to a specific location. He didn't want the drones muddling the circumstances.

"Command for Hammer Six," Yarrow said over the IR link.

"Hammer Six, go."

"Sweep of the sector is complete, no movement. Sending the drones around for a second pass. Expect weather to abate soon. Less rain, more humidity."

"Pass the word, forecast is for less rain. No contact with the Beast."

"Copy that," Booker said then sent the message down the line. A series of thumbs-ups came back to acknowledge everyone had got the word.

Hoffman climbed a moss-covered boulder and checked his team. Barely visible, they moved through a landscape that alternated between intense sunlight and shadows cast by ancient swamp trees. Branches and vines thick as his forearm sagged into the greenish muck.

"What the hell!" Garrison jumped half out of the water, creating a cacophony of splashing noises.

Opal froze, aiming his oversized gauss rifle at the drones buzzing just over their heads. "Opal not scared of drones."

Garrison slipped back into the slimy goo. "I knew that."

Hoffman made eye contact with King at the rear of the column—easier now that the rain had let up—and with a quick hand signal, he initiated phase two of the plan.

"Booker, pass the word. Stage the batteries and set the timers."

Local wildlife squawked as the sun's rays broke through clouds. Booker and Gor'al relieved Garrison and Opal, who moved back to join Max. They checked each of the improvised devices and loaded them into Opal's backpack. The batteries were heavy and had been spread throughout the team. Opal was the only one who could carry them all at once. Garrison and Max quietly argued about details of their placement.

"Duke…" Hoffman started to say.

"Way ahead of you, LT. Just give me a minute to

shimmy up the slip-n-slide tree trunk. It's got at least one good branch for someone of my particular talents…if I can magic myself up there." He spat an impressive stream of chewing tobacco away from the team. "Been holding that for a bit."

"You're disgusting as ever," Booker said, her voice carrying across the still water.

"Stay alert; this might work quicker than we think," Hoffman said.

"I'm up," Duke huffed, slightly out of breath. "Got a pretty good view. There's a clearing ahead; wasn't so sure about it until the mist cleared. Humidity would've been a problem with the antique boomstick you forced on me during round one. I can't wait to put Ice Claw on this freak."

Garrison and Max set the first three devices carefully, strategically placing them where they wanted the Beast to attack. Hoffman felt vulnerable as the drones made another pass. The creature was designed to destroy technology and his support team was pushing the limits from their cozy bunker. He'd seen the devastation the Beast had wrought through the city before the colonists realized how dangerous their modern tech was to themselves.

"We got the main battery packs set," Garrison said. "I—"

The breacher disappeared from view, splashing into the swamp with more noise and commotion than the place had probably seen for a thousand years.

"Max! Grab him before he sinks!" Hoffman rushed forward, creating waves in the stagnant water and risking his own plunge into a hole. He couldn't determine if the comm specialist heard him. Garrison was less and less visible as his silhouette did some kind of arrhythmic interpretive dance under the surface.

"Max! Pull him out!"

"Sir, yes sir!"

A second later, Max and Garrison floundered away from a thick serpent.

"No drown," Opal said, hastily hanging his backpack on the tree higher than any of them could reach. He marched forward, twisting his upper body from side to side to gain momentum as he pushed through the water. The freakishly huge constrictor snake slithered past him and he ignored it until it turned and wrapped around his leg. He punched it in the head. "Snake go away."

Hoffman pulled his bayonet from its sheath and changed course, rushing toward his big friend.

The green and blue snake wrapped around the doughboy's waist and shoulders and slid under his chin for a throat restraint.

Opal grabbed the head with one hand and the main body of the snake with the other and pulled. Blood spurted across the water as the serpent's body thrashed away from him.

"Hate to break this to you, team," Duke said, "but those aren't snakes like you're used to. Looks like they travel in some kind of pack. I have eyes on at least three or four inbound by the water disturbance."

"I think that's called a bed of snakes…or maybe a knot," King said, moving forward to get in line against the attack.

Booker's voice squeaked in a way none of them had ever heard. "Yeah, I don't think you call them a pack. Permission to throw a frag grenade?"

"Duke, can you take care of this?" Hoffman asked.

Opal struggled against a larger, meaner serpent. "Snake no bite Opal!" He punched the creature in the head to make it release, then he choked it with one hand, causing its three-inch fangs to tremble and spew venom. Tendrils of the doughboy's thick green blood splattered across him and his attacker.

A third snake lunged out of the water, causing

Hoffman to stumble backward in surprise. The speed and momentum of these things were incredible. He took a shot but only hit part of the snake's body—with little effect.

"Duke!"

Duke's antique rifle boomed three times, then two times, then once more. Despite the noise and chaos, Hoffman thought he heard the man working the bolt of the old weapon.

"Sorry, I had to switch weapons."

Headless snake bodies drifted away on the water, carried by currents Hoffman hadn't realized were there.

"Hot damn, that was some precision shooting," Garrison panted.

"Taught him everything he knows," Booker said. "It's all breath control."

"Too much noise," King said. He rallied the team, checked everyone for injuries, and inspected their equipment. "Let's move. This train's already ten minutes late."

"Moving to plan B for deployment of the bait batteries," Garrison said.

"What's plan B?" King asked as Hoffman and Booker looked on with interest. Max had a confused look on his face despite his alleged involvement with this scheme.

"Come on, Max. You remember plan B," Garrison said, running to a rock and jamming one of the improvised devices into a crevice. "Opal, hit me."

The doughboy removed one of the batteries, heavy enough to sprain the wrist of an unwary handler, and spiraled it like a football to Garrison, who caught it against his chest and grunted.

"Nice, Opie. You're getting better." Garrison chucked the device into the branches, where it wedged against something unseen.

"Right! Plan B." Max grabbed a battery pack and

lobbed it into a different tree. He glanced at Hoffman. "Plan B's kind of a standard template. I forgot."

"Outstanding. Let's keep moving. We can deploy as we go. This zone's pretty hot. Hopefully, we'll survive the local wildlife long enough to take out the real threat. I'm shutting down my IR link to the drones for now," Hoffman said.

"There's what passes for dry ground in this place about three hundred meters ahead on a bearing of two hundred eighty degrees," Duke said. "I'm coming down. Should reach King's position momentarily."

Stopping the team to give his sniper a chance to catch up, Hoffman looked at his watch. The windup device had a short arm and a long arm that turned clockwise and to one side was a compass dial. "This feels like doing algebra on an abacus."

Booker checked her wrist. "I'm with you. The sooner we take this thing out, the sooner the universe will be aligned in the proper order. Navigation HUDs, power-enhanced armor, and climate control for everyone."

Three flares went up from the tree line. The team stopped and King took tactical command, calling out sectors of fire to the Marines.

Hoffman activated the IR with the drones and radioed the event. "Command, this is Hammer Six. We have three flares four hundred meters ahead of our coordinates on a heading of two hundred sixty-five degrees."

"Acknowledged, Hammer Six."

"Duke, do you have a shot?"

"I might have, if I'd stayed in the tree. There's another perch I can get to, but it'll take me a minute," the sniper said, already heading across a dubious sandbar to an ancient tree that looked like it was sinking at its roots.

"Opal, help him up."

The doughboy charged across the water, glancing

around for snakes and other swamp things. "Opal help!"

"Hold on, let me set down the excess gear," Duke said as he loosened one of his packs.

Opal grabbed him and threw him up, gear and all. The sniper twisted like he was trying to do a cartwheel in midair and landed more or less on one leg and shoulder, gripping the thick branch arms. "I'm…up. Give me a second to acquire the target."

Drones fell out of the sky and crashed through the jungle canopy. Hoffman ripped the IR link from his ear and smashed it with the butt of his rifle.

"This is it, team, the big dance. Prepare to charge your gauss weapons. I think you got that little bugger, LT." King cringed as snakes, frogs, birds, and other less Earth-like analogs fled over the Strike Marine's position.

"You can never be too sure with these gizmos," Hoffman said.

Each member of the team put away antique

weapons and uncased gauss rifles. Hoffman arranged his charge packs for quick reloading, shifting them to the front of his tactical harness, then held one in his hand, ready to slam it into action. Something roared as it approached.

Hoffman shifted his position to get a better look.

"It's big," King said. "I'd say like a lizard-cat out of a mad scientist's laboratory."

"You're not wrong. How long before the batteries activate and really piss it off?" Hoffman checked his watch and tried to ignore the additional slime that had worked its way into his boot. If he wasn't careful, he was going to need sick call when this was over.

"A few minutes, depending on the Beast. We've seen it circle and harass our position—which isn't what we want." The gunnery sergeant stalked toward a downed tree and leaned against it to aim his rifle toward the shape he'd seen a moment before. One by one, the Marines tweaked their positions, looking for the best angle to fire on the expected attack.

Hoffman noted Duke's location—in the only tree large enough to support him. "Give me an update, Duke."

"One moment." The sniper's words were stretched out over several seconds, a sure sign he was searching for something through his optics.

The first battery snapped on—Hoffman heard the distinctive pop of power surging through a cold cell. Two more went live on opposite sides of the bog.

"It's about to get real," King whispered into the sudden silence.

Garrison crouched near the expected point of contact. "Now it's creepy. You with me, Opie?"

"Get ready," Duke said, his words stretching out like an instructor on the range. "Shooters on the line, get your charge packs for reloading because you're about to need them. Don't waste time on low-power shots."

Hoffman lifted the heavy magazine to the bottom of

his weapon, lining it up with the insertion slot. The slight current of the swamp water surged in the opposite direction. It was a subtle, almost noiseless event, but it sent chills up his spine.

"Duke, give me an update," Hoffman said.

"It's a sneaky rascal, but I think we got its attention," Duke said as the rest of the batteries hummed to life.

The Beast exploded through the perimeter. Water fountained into the air as a sickly, mostly rotten tree exploded. The densely muscled creature charged forward, chomping with jaws spread wide as a small ground car. It slashed wicked claws through the air, shredding another swamp tree, the hanging vines spiraling into the air from the force of the impact. The creature surged into and out of the water like a killer whale on the hunt.

Two of the bait batteries disappeared in the furious attack. The Beast hesitated, turning to face a half-dozen new power flares.

Hoffman rammed the battery into his gauss rifle and activated the weapon. He felt a thrum of electricity travel through the magnetic coils and a charge indicator near the rear sight turned on. The gauge filled—very, very slowly.

In the distance, the Beast froze. Its triangular head lifted up and twisted to look straight at Hoffman through the jungle.

"Ah crap," Garrison said, slapping the side of his gauss rifle, encouraging it to charge faster.

"Suppressing fire!" King shouted as he, Booker, and Max opened up with their gauss weapons on low power, sending up a quick hail of magnetically accelerated bolts.

The difference between gauss fire and regular bullets was stunning. He felt like a kid who had never seen fireworks. Trees exploded. Shredded wood and vegetation blasted in all directions. Rounds hit the water and sent up plumes of steam.

The Beast turned away from its stationary quarry and rushed Hoffman's team, its bottom row of eyes flashing wide while the others narrowed and scanned side to side. A hunk of bark dropped from its wide mouth. It drove forward through the swamp with explosive acceleration that Hoffman couldn't believe.

"Reloading!" Garrison shouted. "Just as fast…as possible." His voice went up two octaves.

"Firing! You're out already?" Booker said as an afterthought, her attention clearly on the task at hand. "OK, now I'm reloading."

"I cannot believe it is still coming," Steuben growled between shots.

Duke's voice, normally calmer during a fight than it was in everyday conversation, blasted through the IR comms—which they were using now that they had provoked the Beast and didn't need to worry about drawing its attention. "Shift fire! Shift fire! It's right on top of Opal."

Hoffman saw the doughboy swing his huge hammer and shouted, echoing his sniper, "Shift fire! Friendly in the kill zone!" He moved his point-of-aim a few meters ahead of Opal's attacker, anticipating its next move.

"Break you!" Opal swung with both hands, striking it firmly on the bridge of its nasal plate. The wedge-shaped head didn't really have a nose, but rather wide openings that reminded Hoffman of a supercharger's air intake port, the only difference being the thick organic film that lined the creature's eyes, nose, and mouth.

"No!" Opal roared as it smashed him sideways, slashing with its teeth and claws. Opal threw up a hammer to block the blow as he fell beneath the water and was pressed deeper by the second and third sets of legs.

"Did you see that? It just ran over Opie. Opie! Nobody knocks down a doughboy like that," Garrison shouted, ripping off rounds faster and faster. "Give me back my doughboy, you freak!"

Hoffman still couldn't see the Beast in its entirety and feared it would just keep coming and coming. It was bigger than he thought and a hell of a lot faster. He knew it had been struck several times with gauss rounds and thought he'd seen it flinch.

Hoffman checked his charge indicator: still several seconds away from a high-powered shot.

Opal crawled out of the swamp, heading straight for his hammer, and Duke fired Ice Claw. The rail rifle split the air with a sonic boom as a hypervelocity round sliced through the air, leaving a trail of burning oxygen in its wake.

The concussion from the rail shot shoved Hoffman into a tree and his ears rang.

Matte-black armor plates sprang into the air as the round drilled through the Beast's shoulder, slamming the creature into the swamp like a giant boot had stepped on it. It lay still as water rushed over it. Alien flesh and slime fountained near the thing's neck as the round zipped through and out the other side.

"Bang out!" Garrison shouted, heaving a bomb with all his strength. The team dove to the ground, scrambling for cover. A second later, an explosion shook the jungle.

Hoffman stumbled to his feet and aimed his fully charged gauss rifle at a black mass in the water. He pulled the trigger and, for a second, nothing happened until searing heat spread through his hands and he threw the weapon aside. The battery pack glowed red-hot and popped, flipping the rifle into a puddle. The rest of the Marines had dropped their rifles as well.

"Bad," Gor'al said, drawing his old-style assault rifle off his back. "This is very bad."

In the swamp, the black mass of the Beast slunk away from the Marines.

"Orbital strike?" King asked. "We hurt it, at least."

"Time to finish the job." Hoffman removed a second IR transmitter from his belt and plugged a battery into it.

"We need to keep line of sight on the Beast," Hoffman said. "Orbital strikes have room for error, but I don't trust the Navy."

King pointed off to the left. "If we can get across this field of mush, there's hardcover over there. I see at least three boulders that must be sitting on solid ground. Beast's swimming around it all."

Hoffman held his position until his team was set, then sprinted toward them. "Moving!" Sliding behind a swamp boulder, he said, "Duke, time for the big gun."

Duke fired twice in rapid succession, slamming rounds into its shoulder, stopping it dead in its tracks. "When you want something done right…"

Hoffman stared at the floundering monster. "What

are you waiting for? Do it again."

Duke fired three rounds, each a second apart and well-placed into the armored shoulder girdle of the thing. The kinetic force staggered it.

"Keep running!" Garrison said. "Haven't I taught you people anything?"

King turned and fled. "As much as I hate to admit it, I agree with Garrison on this one. Team, let's get outta here. Fight another day."

Hoffman looked down at the assault rifle he knew was barely effective against the Beast. But if they had the creature hurt and near death, then they might still have a chance to finish it off.

He put the IR transmitter into his ear. "Talk to me, Duke."

"Had to hot swap my battery," Duke said. "Ready to fire in forty-five seconds."

"You get eyes on the target, you call in an orbital

strike to finish it off," Hoffman said.

"Kind of pushing 'danger close' to a whole new level, LT."

"Eyes open." Hoffman closed the channel and linked up with the rest of the team in the middle of several boulders. "Where is it?"

"Negative contact." Steuben lifted his head slightly. "I still can't smell it."

"No eyes on," Garrison said, peeking around a boulder. No one else could see the Beast either.

Hoffman looked back to Duke's tree, and an empty pit formed in his stomach.

****

"I need a raise," Duke muttered the moment he unkeyed his IR comm. He spat dip spit over the side of his perch, feeling the humidity stick to his skin. The air was so still, he wasn't sure this environment was real. How lucky would it be to suddenly have a sniper's wet dream once the humidity and local gravity was factored into his range calculations? He should've been set up somewhere he could see for miles, not a spot the instructors at Sniper School would've laughed at him for choosing.

The sounds of trees smashing behind him caught his attention. Duke frowned then remembered the other batteries on timers he and the team had seeded behind them. There was a roar and a shadow passed between trees, moving straight for him.

"Ah…shit…" Duke pulled the IR transmitter from his ear and flung it away, holding very still as the Beast emerged from the water, electricity crackling around a crater in its shoulder where Duke had hit it. The creature moved stiffly as its head swept from side to side over the swamp.

Duke reached onto the small of his back to the

battery pack that powered his rail rifle and clicked the charge lever to DRAIN, feeling Ice Claw grow colder against his cheek. He slipped his hand into a pouch and removed a metal pin the length of a finger.

He'd heard of an old trick from Strike Marine sniper lore but never tested it. Something a hero of the Ember War had improvised on the battlefield. He pushed the pin into a port on the side of the battery pack and electricity zapped his fingers, leaving them numb.

The Beast's head angled up, then swung toward Duke.

"Yeah, you see me." Duke swallowed hard. "What're you going to do about it, ugly?"

The Beast's claws gripped the muck, then it sprang toward Duke's tree.

He pulled the emergency release cord on the battery pack and tossed the overheating pack up into the higher branches. Gripping Ice Claw, he looked down to see the

Beast slam its talons into the bark and climb straight for him.

"Fuuu—" Duke leapt out of the tree just as the Beast roared past him, landing on his side in the muck, knocking all the wind out of him. He clutched his sniper rifle to his chest and rolled into a stream.

The Beast bit down on the battery pack just as the cascading storage failure he initiated with the sabotage reached critical. The pack exploded with a fireball, annihilating the upper half of the tree and sending flaming chunks of wood out like shrapnel from an artillery strike.

Duke felt the concussion through the water and had a half second to realize he was being swept toward a rock. He managed to take the blow on the head and shoulder, protecting Ice Claw with his body. The hit sent a flash across his eyes and his body went loose. He felt like drifting away, surrendering to the quiet of the dark, when his rifle just barely slipped from his fingers.

Snapping back, Duke thrashed around, one foot hitting the weapon. He twisted over and grabbed one of the twin acceleration vanes, feeling it cut into the flesh of his hand as he kicked against the current, not sure which way was up.

Something gripped his ankle, and he realized one of those anaconda-analogs must have survived. With a yank against his leg, he was out of the water, hanging upside down as mud and silt-laden water poured off his body and across his face.

"My…my…" he sputtered, clutching his weapon against his body and kicking feebly. "My dip!"

"Told you he looked fine," Max said.

Duke got one eye clear and saw Opal holding him up like a freshly caught fish.

"Put him down," Booker said and Opal let Duke flop to the ground.

"Did I get it?" Duke asked, face down in the mud.

"Look," Hoffman said as he slapped the sniper on the shoulder and pointed ahead of them. He craned his neck up and saw a hunk of the Beast's leg embedded in a tree trunk, smoking. Duke flopped his head back into the muck.

"I hate this planet," Duke groaned as Booker rolled him over and shined a light in his eye. "Hate hunting. Where's my dip? Don't let that thieving Dotty get it…"

"He's got another concussion," Booker said. "Lacerations to the scalp and face. Still ugly and stupid."

"Is she OK?" Duke asked, running his hands down his rifle and breathing a sigh of relief.

"He was *not* this concerned when I got shot," Max said.

"Movement!" Steuben shouted.

Duke tried to react as Marine weapons opened fire. He got to one knee, brought his sniper rifle up, and then lost his balance as the world went spinning. He fell on his side and laughed weakly. Looking up, he saw the hunk of the Beast was gone.

"It…came back for its leg?" Duke asked.

"It's gone…" Hoffman said, putting a hand to Duke's chest to keep him from getting up again.

"Grendel's mother came for it." Duke raised a finger. "Call me Beowulf…'cause that's who I am!"

"Severe concussion." Booker shook her head.

"We've done what we can." Hoffman pulled Duke up and threw his arm over his shoulder. "Return to base. I'll call in a strike on this area soon as we're clear."

"My legs are all funny," Duke said, slumping between Hoffman and Garrison as the breacher took the other shoulder.

"Let me carry that." Gor'al reached for Ice Claw, but Duke managed a weak kick to the Dotari's thigh.

"Hands off, dip thief!"

Duke kept hold of the rail rifle as the Strike Marines marched out of the jungle.

Chapter 14

Hoffman helped Duke into the bed of a cargo truck and climbed in after him. He swung the flap up, kicked the bed twice, and the truck lurched forward in a cloud of exhaust.

His team was muddy, beaten, and exhausted, but they were all there and they were alive. He set the muzzle of his rifle against the side of his foot and pulled a data slate from a pack. Knocking some mud off it, he switched on his IR transmitter.

"Hammer Six to Command, we need to break contact. Mission success in doubt."

"What happened?" Colonel Fallon appeared on the data slate.

Hoffman gave a quick recap of the battle in the swamp as thunder from distant orbital kinetic strikes echoed through the city.

"It was hit by a rail rifle and then blown to pieces," Yarrow said, coming onscreen with Fallon, "then it…reformed?"

"Our best guess," Hoffman said. "This isn't any flesh-and-blood creature we're dealing with, at least not one we've dealt with before. It appears a good deal more resilient than the Xaros drones we've fought before."

"That explains why it has no scent," Steuben said. "It isn't alive."

"It may be pure Qa'Resh tech," Yarrow said, stroking his goatee. "But if it's inorganic, that may be a weakness. It's like fighting the Xaros drones all over again."

An idea formed in the back of Hoffman's mind.

"Armor was effective," Steuben said, "but the Beast can shut them down in a—"

"Wait, wait," Hoffman said as he held up a hand. "What was that munition we had when the Xaros put siege to Earth? You both used it in that stupid movie."

"I told you never to discuss that abomination," Steuben said.

"Quadrium?" Yarrow asked. "Quadrium…it disrupted the drone's control systems, left them vulnerable and stunned. That…that could work."

"Don't suppose you have any of those silver bullets lying around," Fallon said.

"We have an omnium factory. We can have anything we need in a few hours." Yarrow picked up a data slate and began tapping quickly.

"Get your Marines seen by the docs and get prepped to go out again," the colonel said. "You may not feel like this was a win, Hoffman, but you've got us one step closer to victory. Fallon out."

The screen cut off.

Hoffman let his head bounce against the back of the truck's side rails and released a slow breath.

"This thing was made to stop the Xaros invasion," Hoffman said. "We're just a handful of Devil Dogs with a mean streak."

"You seem less than confident," Steuben said.

Hoffman looked over at his Marines, who all were focused on Duke.

"Not too long ago, we were stuck in deep space on a Dotari ship full of Banshees trying to kill us…" Hoffman felt an ache in his chest from the sutures that had closed up his wound.

"You'd rather be back there?" Steuben asked.

"I know how that turned out. This is an open-ended mess. Was it ever this bad back when you were with Hale and on the *Breitenfeld*?" Hoffman felt a pang, mentioning the captured ship.

"The past has already been won or lost, Marine," said Steuben. "This hunt will only end with us dead or victorious. Hale and Valdar looked at the fight as a struggle against extinction for all of humanity. What will happen if we fail here?"

Hoffman half smiled. "Who knows if what's in that lab will turn the tide?"

"And if it does?"

Hoffman leaned forward and brushed grime from the stubble on his scalp. "Then this will be the most pivotal battle in the war against the Kesaht."

"I went to Anthalas with Hale and Valdar. We did not know what we would find…but there we brought back the key to our final victory over the Xaros and set in motion events that led to my people being rescued and the Toth nearly annihilated. It was a good day."

"Hindsight, eh?"

"Every fight matters, Hoffman. Every fight."

"Hale made you his executive officer down the line, didn't he?"

Steuben nodded

"Smart move," Hoffman said as the adrenaline wore off and his injuries made themselves known.

The truck turned a corner to a hospital.

"Hey!" Duke pointed over one side. "Look at that penguin!"

"Where?" Gor'al twisted onto his feet and peeked over the rails. "What is a penguin? Are they dangerous?"

Duke reached into Gor'al's cargo pocket and pulled out two cans of dip.

"I knew it! Taking dip off a wounded Marine." Duke kicked the Dotari in the hip.

"Never! I stole those two wintergreen cans from you months ago. You only had peach blend and menthol in your pack when we went into the jungle," Gor'al said, wagging a finger at Duke.

The sniper looked at the cans, then tapped them with his fingertips. "Oh," Duke said and slipped the cans into his pocket.

"Then give those back!" Gor'al's quills flared.

"You said you stole them from me," Duke huffed.

"No, I meant to say I was holding them for you. In case of an emergency. Like this one. Enjoy them. Yes. That's what I meant," Gor'al said.

"Are they always like this?" Steuben asked Hoffman quietly.

"Duke's going to start nabbing Gor'al's coffee beans before too long. Dotari get a buzz off those too," Hoffman said.

"Could be worse. Standish would steal anything that wasn't nailed down, which was useful when we needed parts and equipment."

"Don't give them any ideas, yeah?" Hoffman rubbed a cramp out of a thigh as the truck stopped outside the emergency room.

Chapter 15

Lilith hadn't been sleeping at her desk. Professionals didn't do that. She'd merely been resting her eyes. Everyone else had gone to their quarters hours ago, so why shouldn't she rest her eyes?

The analog phone on her desk rang. She stared at it, not sure how to interpret the harsh bell. A sip of cold coffee restored a portion of her analytic abilities and she lifted the receiver to her ear.

"Hello, Lilith, Lab 1, speaking."

"Oh, good. I'm so glad you answered. Do you have a team with you right now? One of the devices has activated."

"Who is this?" Lilith asked.

"Masha. You remember me? The one you educated on spotting Qa'Resh fakes. I'm at Lab 3 on the south side."

"Yes, of course. No one's here. They're trying to sleep…like I should be. What's going on?"

"I'm not exactly sure. It isn't doing much, but…I was practicing some of the authentication scans you taught me and it started giving a power signature. I sent it to you through the tubes."

Lilith almost dropped the phone. "You did what? You put an active device in the tubes?"

"You make it sound like a bad thing…"

Lilith whacked the receiver against the desk twice. "Yes, it is a bad thing, you—you know what? I'll go get the device and you better pray to all the gods that it isn't damaged. You're going on report for a handling violation and you'll be digging ditches by morning. I know the right people to make that happen." She slammed the phone down and stormed out of her office, mumbling curses from several different languages.

Entering the tube room, Lilith came to a sudden stop. The large tube hatch was open, a canister waiting inside.

"What the—"

The door slammed shut and pain erupted against Lilith's kidneys as a Taser jammed into her lab coat. Lilith went down with a pathetic cry. Masha tightened a zip tie onto Lilith's wrists and put a knee to her sternum. With a hand over Lilith's mouth, she shushed her.

"Your employment situation has changed," Masha said. "*I* am not a lab flunky. *I* am an agent of the Ibarran Nation and if you—"

Lilith tried to shout and squirm away, but Masha kept a firm grip over her mouth.

"Scream and your husband will die," Masha said.

"Think I'm kidding?"

Lilith's eyes went wide.

"There's a small explosive device in the command center. Two pounds of denethrite explosive in the base of the coffee maker. Doesn't sound like much, but denethrite's a mean little bugger. Six ounces can take out the whole floor. Two pounds is just too much, but when I need to make a point, I'm not one for subtlety. Savvy?"

Lilith stared daggers at the spy.

"Up down? Left right?" Masha asked.

Lilith nodded.

Masha turned her arm around and showed an analog watch face to Lilith. "In two hours and…thirty-nine minutes, that bomb will go off. We can reach my ship in two hours. Soon as we're there, I'll tell your hubby about the bomb and everyone will live to see tomorrow. Sound fun?"

Lilith mumbled against Masha's palm.

"No screaming," Masha said. "If you make a scene…" She flourished one hand and a knife appeared. "You die and no one at HQ has a chance."

Masha took her hand away.

"The Beast is out there. There's no way you'll make it to your ship," Lilith said.

"I'll worry about the Beast. You worry about being a good little helper for the Ibarra Nation. Because if you are anything but a peppy little go-getter, my agents on Eridu will see that your husband has an unfortunate—but very fatal—accident. Same with your daughter Mary on Barnard's Star," Masha said.

"You wouldn't. If you hurt them, I'll never help you."

"I'm willing to bet your maternal instincts are stronger than your loyalty to whoever signs your paycheck. You wouldn't believe what Lady Ibarra's learned about the Qa'Resh since she left the traitors in the Union. Not at all a bit curious what she's up to?"

"My husband. Tell them about the bomb before—"

"Time-conscious and goal-oriented. I like that." Masha wrapped a gag around the bottom of Lilith's face. "You get to ride the tubes first. I hear it's a bit bumpy, but what're you going to do, eh?"

Masha hauled Lilith up and manhandled her into the canister.

****

A truck chugged down a road, the engine straining as the transmission chugged from one gear to another. It jumped a curb and came to a stop outside the entrance to a tube station, where dozens on top of dozens of pneumatic lines rose out of the ground and plugged into one wall of the structure, all evenly spaced.

The passenger side door flew open and Max almost fell from the cab.

"You are fired as driver!" he yelled.

Opal squeezed out to stand next to Max. The doughboy scanned the nearby buildings, eyes lingering over the setting sun.

"What?" Garrison stood up from the driver's side and waved a hand at Max as the truck rolled forward. Garrison ducked back inside and the emergency brake cranked. The Marine got out and brushed his hands against his fatigues.

"And you're fired as navigator," Garrison said.

"So what if I'm used to just plugging an address into a car's auto-drive and sitting back?" Max asked. "I got us here, didn't I? You're the one that has to explain all the new dents."

"Dents?" Garrison glanced at the beat-up bumper. "What new dents?"

"Garrison hit two parked cars," Opal said. "Three concrete obstacles. One—"

"They jumped in front of me! And those dents were

there when we got the keys."

"Garrison hit—"

"They were there when we got the keys!" Garrison wagged a finger at the doughboy. "Now let's get inside and get those quadriceps rounds or whatever the LT said we need to mess up the Beast. Yeah? Better idea than sitting out here and laying blame for something that didn't even happen."

He motioned toward a loading dock and walked off.

"Don't understand," Opal said to Max.

"You don't have a paycheck to dock, big guy," Max said. "Just smile and nod if anyone asks about damage to the truck."

Opal pulled his lips back to reveal slab-like teeth and bobbed his head up and down.

"Or not. Because that wouldn't beg more questions from King or any of the REMFs on this rock." Max pushed a double door open and whistled as he looked at the tube station.

Pneumatic tubes the size of coffins were laid out across the main floor, and stacks and stacks of smaller canisters were in racks against the walls. A skeleton of catwalks and exposed lifts were built into the receiving wall.

"My grandma told me stories about old-school office buildings and hospitals," Max said. "How they'd shuffle around paperwork and stuff. Before everything went digital."

"We're looking for tube AA-92 through 96," Garrison said. "Should have our Q-shells and new gauss weapons so we can fight like almost-proper Marines."

"Ninety-five," Max said, slapping a palm against a large canister and flipping up the lid. "Gauss rifles. Check." He struggled to pull a case out then called Opal over.

"I don't see the others." Garrison put his hands on his hips and stared at the racks of smaller canisters. "Bet our needle's in that haystack. Figures."

He went up a set of stairs to the lowest receiving platform and made his way down the corrugated metal path, glancing at the tubes in the bays.

"B-92, C-17," Garrison read as he went. "You'd think they'd have someone here to help, but sunset is the new pumpkin-time for Eridu and—"

Warning lights flashed at an empty cradle just ahead of Garrison and a tube clattered to a stop.

"Think we're that lucky?" Garrison asked Max, who was leaving the building with his arms full of a gauss ammo pallet.

Garrison fumbled around with the cradle's controls before it opened with a hiss of hydraulics. The Marine looked over the canister and cursed.

Another empty cradle announced an imminent arrival.

"Of course the marker's on the other side," he

muttered, putting his hands against the canister and rotating it. A window came into view, and Garrison pressed his face to it. He put a hand next to his eyes to block the lights and saw a woman inside, her hands bound and mouth gagged.

"What in the hell?" He pulled back and looked to the door, but neither Max nor Opal had returned. "Hey! Get back here!"

He jiggled the slide on the window and got it open. "You OK? Hey, you're Lilith Yarrow." Garrison reached into the window and Lilith responded, her speech muffled as she gestured wildly with her cuffed hands.

"I don't speak mumble." Garrison pulled the gag out of Lilith's mouth.

"She's here! She's here!" Lilith shouted, eyes wide.

"Who? Why can't anything ever be easy on this planet?" Garrison grabbed Lilith by the shoulders to pull her out when he heard a pistol's hammer lock back.

"Who else is with you?" a familiar voice asked

from behind.

Garrison froze, acutely aware that he did not have a weapon on him. He turned his head slowly and found Masha behind him, pistol leveled at his face. He brought his hands out and raised them next to his head.

"You…" Garrison's eyes narrowed. "I owe you."

"Yes, me," Masha said. "I really did not want to meet up with you Jarheads again. I know we had a bad parting on Koen, but we can move beyond that, yeah?"

Garrison's eyes darted to the doors that Opal and Max would come through any second.

"You tasered me and locked me in a cell," Garrison said, his focus back on Masha.

"I was being nice and I did mention you'd die if you—or any of Hoffman's lackeys—got in my way again."

"You're stalling." Garrison's eyes narrowed.

"So are you." Masha half turned her head to the door then snapped her gaze back to Garrison as he leaned his weight forward to the balls of his feet.

"She's after the artifacts in the lab," Lilith said. "There's a—"

"Shut up!" Masha took a step to one side. "You. Knuckle-dragger. Hands interlaced behind your head and on your knees. Now."

The double doors opened, distracting Masha for a split second, and Garrison struck out with one palm, twisting his body out of her line of fire. His hand struck the Ibarran spy's wrist and sent the pistol flying.

Garrison, off-balance, tried to grab Masha's sleeve, but she yanked it away and stepped closer to him, jabbing him in the throat. Garrison made a noise between a gag and a choke as her shin connected square against his crotch and his feet lifted off the ground.

He went down in a heap of pain, eyes watering and lungs refusing to breathe. He heard shouting and two gunshots before he managed a ragged breath and looked up.

He saw Masha's feet running away, a second pair of boots keeping pace with her.

"Garrison, you OK?" Max yelled from behind a canister.

Garrison waved at Masha and gagged.

"Was that who I think it was?" Max asked.

Garrison gagged a bit louder then collapsed against the ground, pain radiating from his testicles and his throat. Just which was worse would change as time went on. He looked at the doors and wondered, *Where the hell is Opal?*

****

Opal sprinted down the outside of the tube station. He turned his momentum into a slide as he came around a corner, careening into a pile of broken canisters around a dumpster. A ground car, its headlights on, was parked in the alley, trunk open.

Masha stood behind the open passenger door, her jaw loose as she saw the doughboy.

"Oh...*arraio*." She swallowed hard. "Medvedev, this one's for you, my love."

The trunk slammed shut and an Ibarran legionnaire in work overalls swung a rifle over the top of the car.

Opal swiped a hand against the broken canisters and shot one straight at Medvedev. It whacked against the barrel and deflected the shot just enough to miss Opal's face by a fraction of an inch.

The doughboy crouched low and charged. His shoulder hit the car and pushed it back a yard, knocking Medvedev off his feet and sending him into the alley wall.

Masha yelped and ducked into the car. Opal slammed her door shut and went for Medvedev.

The legionnaire was big by human standards—six and a half feet tall and built like a professional fighter—but he didn't have Opal's mass or the taller battle construct's reach. Medvedev popped to his feet and slipped something out from beneath his belt. He flipped a switchblade open and held the knife out, his other hand up near his face.

"I've been waiting for this," Medvedev said. "Your programming keep you from killing me?"

"Can hurt you." Opal feinted a punch and got Medvedev to swipe the blade through air. The doughboy jabbed again and caught Medvedev on the shoulder. The legionnaire ducked and kicked Opal in his leading knee, shifting him off-balance.

"No time for this!" Masha crawled out of the car and went for the rifle.

Medvedev stabbed his weapon toward Opal's heart, but Opal caught him by the wrist. Medvedev tried to yank his hand back, but Opal's grip held. Opal swung a haymaker at the man's face but missed as Medvedev dove forward.

Opal kept his grip and the legionnaire's momentum

pulled him off-balance and against Medvedev's leg. The doughboy tripped forward and went face-first into the side of the car, letting go of the wrist.

Swinging a blind fist, Opal caught Medvedev's forearm raised in a block. The doughboy pivoted to one side as the switchblade ripped across his torso, tearing his fatigues and cutting flesh. Opal punched Medvedev in the jaw and sent him sprawling.

Opal reached down and snatched Masha by the calf as she reached for the rifle. He yanked her back, whacked her against the front tire, then turned back to Medvedev just as the man threw the switchblade at Opal's face. Opal raised a palm and the knife buried itself up to the hilt in his flesh, the knifepoint a half inch from Opal's eye.

Medvedev kicked Opal in the stomach, doubling him over. He smashed an elbow into the doughboy's nose then landed an uppercut to Opal's chin, snapping his head back.

"Not so tough," Medvedev said as he chopped a hand against Opal's neck and the doughboy fell against the car.

"Old." Medvedev slammed a fist into Opal's ribs. "Obsolete. Tra—"

Opal caught Medvedev's fist and growled. Rearing his head back, Opal slammed his forehead into Medvedev's face. He gripped the legionnaire by the neck with one hand, squeezing until the man couldn't breathe and blood stopped flowing to his brain.

"Go sleep," Opal said.

Medvedev slapped at Opal's arm weakly, his consciousness fleeing.

"Opie! Hey, Opie," Masha called, holding up a small video tablet in one hand. "Got something for you."

Grainy footage of a man with permed hair and a wide-collared shirt standing in front of a half-finished painting played on the screen.

"Mix up a little more color here, then we can put us a little shadow right in there. See how you can move things around?" the man said with a kind voice.

Opal let Medvedev go and his eyes went soft.

"Happy little trees. Right, Opal?" Masha asked.

"They didn't adjust your programming after our last run in? Sloppy. You tell Hoffman I remember my enemy's weaknesses."

Medvedev coughed and picked up his rifle.

The other doors burst open and Garrison and Max froze in the threshold as Medvedev brought his rifle up and fired from the hip, shooting through the car's windows and missing the Marines. The two scrambled back into the building as Medvedev put rounds into the walls every few seconds as Masha got the car started.

The legionnaire was still shooting, his body half in and half out of the car as it sped away.

"Opal?" Max called out from the corner. "Opal,

what's wrong with you?"

"There…let's have some more fun. Let's take some black. Some Prussian blue," came from the tablet at Opal's feet. Max peeked quickly around the corner, then ran to Opal. He crushed the tablet with his boot and Opal's head snapped up.

"Bad ones." Opal looked around. "Where?"

Garrison pointed down the alley, croaked, then gestured wildly back to the tube station.

"He's right." Max looked Opal over, concern writ across his face as he examined the blade still stuck in Opal's hand. "We need to get back to Hoffman and tell him about the Ibarrans."

Garrison mimed shooting a gun.

"And the gear." Max looked at the sunset. "Got to hurry. You OK, Opie?"

Opal pulled the switchblade out and tossed it aside.

"Unit functional," Opal said.

"I'm really starting to hate those assholes," Max said. "Let's move."

Chapter 16

Garrison winced as Booker touched his throat with an exam wand.

"It was her, sir," he said hoarsely to Hoffman. "Positive it was Masha and they've got Lilith."

"And Medvedev was there," Max said. "He managed to not shoot my guts out this time, not for lack of trying."

King stood up from a field telephone, the archaic handset against his ear.

"Lieutenant, report from checkpoint seven: a car got through the outer wall. Heading north."

"The gate was open?" Hoffman's brow furrowed.

"Locals say the guards in the tower are dead," King said. "There must be more than two Ibarrans on this planet."

"They have a ship," Steuben said. "That is the only reason they would leave the city."

"If they try and take off anywhere that the Beast can get line of sight on them, it'll fry their systems," Hoffman said. "But the Ibarrans aren't stupid. Can't make the mistake of underestimating them again."

"Ow," Garrison said, pushing Booker's probe away. "Quit it…oh, that is better. How about my balls?"

"Motrin and water," Booker sneered. "You're lucky you got your ass handed to you by a girl, else you'd be in serious pain."

"That stings, corpsman, it really stings," Garrison said as he adjusted the ice pack on his crotch.

A tablet in Hoffman's cargo pocket buzzed. He

whipped it out and a screen of Yarrow and Fallon appeared.

"Sirs," the lieutenant said, "I was just about to call. We've got a situation—"

"My wife is missing," Yarrow said. "Her office was ransacked and—"

"Ibarran agents," Hoffman said. "We've had a run-in with them before. Chances are they're still on world. Last sighting had them moving straight into Beast country."

"That's suicide," Fallon said. "It's nearly dark."

"Assume they have a plan," Hoffman said. "If they had a ship in that jungle, where would it be?"

"They have Yarrow's mate," Steuben said. "She is an expert on Qa'Resh technology, yes? Where is the only other source of that tech on this planet?"

"The lab," Hoffman said. He swiped down on the screen and pulled up a map. "There's a road from checkpoint seven that runs close to the excavation site…if they've been on world since before the Beast woke up, they might have set down near the lab."

"Then we need to get out there, track them," Steuben said.

"How are we going to—?"

Steuben pointed at Garrison. "He bears a scent. So does Opal, one far stronger."

"I keep forgetting you're an amateur bloodhound," Hoffman said.

"Amateur?" Steuben raised an eyebrow.

"I monitored that," Fallon said from the screen. "Get out there and recover Lilith Yarrow. Both that Medvedev and Masha you described are wanted for murder on Mars. Bring them in alive if you can. If not, no complaints."

"There is the Beast," Hoffman said, looking over at the crates Garrison and Max had brought with them.

"We're sending up drones to lure the Beast away," Fallon said. "We can buy you some time. Let's hope the quadrium rounds work as intended."

"I love being the guinea pig," Garrison muttered.

"Roger, sir." Hoffman looked at King. "Gunney, have the team load up. We'll get our gear squared as we move."

"Oorah." King slammed the phone down and ran out of the room.

"Steuben," Yarrow said, "please…it's my wife. My love. You have to get her back."

"I owe you more than that," the Karigole said. "She will return to you. I swear it."

"Garrison, can you drive?" Hoffman asked.

"Sure thing, sir. My lead foot is at the ready." The breacher got up and waddled toward the door, dropping ice cubes from the plastic bag held between his legs.

****

Masha flipped the floodlights on as darkness fell across the jungle. She swerved around a bend, eyes darting from side to side.

Medvedev nursed a sore jaw and dabbed a suture wand at a cut just beneath his eye. Dried blood ran down his cheek and stained his overalls. The car swerved and he poked himself in the temple.

"Let one of them drive," the legionnaire said, glancing up at the rearview mirror. Three more legionnaires in black fatigues were crammed into the backseat, two men and a woman, their face shields adorned with red crusader crosses.

"We can't stop here. This is Beast country," Masha said, "and I don't know about your judgment. Why didn't you shoot the doughboy? You want him to catch up and turn your face into hamburger again?"

"Opal was disabled," Medvedev said. "No longer a threat to us. No honor in killing one that can't fight back.

Besides, if I'd shot him, the other Strike Marines would have had no reason to hang back. We needed the space."

"A doughboy," one of the male legionnaires said.

"They're not to be taken lightly," the female said.

"Masha, you're going to plow into a tree before the Beast finds us," Medvedev said, "which will be sooner than later if the ship didn't get our signal."

"They acknowledged," a female legionnaire said. "Decoy electrical sources are in the air. The lights are concentrated chem-lights, but the noise of the combustion engine is a big 'eat me' sign for the Beast."

"We're almost to the lab," Masha said. "We'll have to go in on foot anyway. Just a quick stop before we leave this Union crap hole."

"We're not going straight to the ship?" Medvedev lowered the suture wand.

"Lady Ibarra sent us here for the asset in the trunk," Masha said. "But she needs Qa'Resh tech, and what's in that lab is worth the risk."

"Our mission—"

"Is half complete with just the scientist," Masha snapped. "You want to return to the Lady in failure? The armor came back from their mission to rescue the last Aeon in shame after they failed. We won't let down the Lady or the Ibarra Nation, will we?"

"The Lady wills it," one of the legionnaires said from the backseat.

"And who are we to question her?" Medvedev said, looking over his shoulder to the female sitting in the middle.

She beat a fist against her heart twice in salute.

"Then we're in agreement," Masha smiled. "And Hoffman and his bunch of meddlesome twits are on our tail. They'll either slow the Beast down or take care of it for us. Win-win for us, any way it works out."

"You have more faith than I do." Medvedev

glanced at a paper map. "There, the next turn. You can see where the Pathfinder vehicle cut through the jungle."

Masha pulled the car onto the shoulder of the road and looked through the thick undergrowth. The Pathfinders traveled in all-terrain vehicles; their car was meant for jaunts over paved roads in a city.

"You guys like walking, right? You're ground pounders. One of you carry Lilith," she said.

****

Garrison pumped the brake as the cargo truck rounded a corner, its headlights sweeping over a car half off the shoulder, the front end buried in reeds.

"Think that's the Ibarrans?" Garrison asked Hoffman, who sat in the front passenger seat.

There were two slaps on the roof.

"The engine is still hot," Steuben shouted.

"Dismount and follow me."

"Aggressive, ain't he?" Garrison shut the truck off and killed the lights.

"When in doubt, attack." Hoffman kicked his door open and hopped out, assault rifle braced against his shoulder. The rest of the team jumped over the rails and formed a quick perimeter.

Steuben sniffed at the air and took off at a quick jog down a pair of beaten foliage paths.

"Those are Pathfinder excursion-vehicle tracks," Max said. "We really need Steuben's nose to follow that?"

"Stow it." King hopped over a ditch and took the other path. "Tactical. Let's move."

Hoffman looked to the horizon as the last band of sunset faded away. They were about to enter the Beast's jungle at night, with no optics and no good idea of where the Beast even was. The weight of an unpowered gauss rifle and quadrium rounds on his belt were little comfort.

"Team," Hoffman said as they moved through the undergrowth, wide fronds and wet leaves sliding across their faces and shoulders as they moved, "Q-shells need a high-power gauss shot to activate. Don't get trigger-happy and waste bullets."

"The Beast will sit still while our batteries spin up, yeah?" Duke asked.

"If it'll sit still, I've got a present for that damn thing," Garrison said, slapping a satchel charge strapped to the small of his back. "Denethrite special. If that doesn't finish it off, I'll turn in my globe and anchor."

"If your toe-popper does anything but blow it to proverbial smithereens, the Beast will probably poop out your globe and anchor at its leisure," Max said.

"Wouldn't that just be the cherry to top my day." Garrison adjusted his crotch. "What's the call on the Ibarrans, Lieutenant?"

"Lilith is the target," Hoffman said. "Don't put her

in any danger if we can help it. The Ibarrans are declared hostiles. Treat them as such."

"Finally," King said. "There's blood between us. Time to make them pay."

Steuben stopped and raised a fist. The Marines went to one knee on either side of the paths, peering into the jungle. Hoffman came up to the Karigole at a crouch.

"What is it?" he asked.

"Do you not hear that?" Steuben flicked a thumb to the sky.

"No…what do you—"

A drone whizzed over the canopy, lights flashing. The crack of breaking wood and shaking branches erupted in the distance, the disturbance cutting across the path a few dozen yards ahead and continuing into the darkness.

"There is the Beast," Steuben said and drew his short scimitar off his back.

"Gauss?" King asked.

"Not yet," Hoffman said. "The drone might lead it away before we—a sword? Really, Steuben?"

"For them," the Karigole said, pointing the blade to the right. Light crept through the jungle from a source Hoffman couldn't quite make out. "The Ibarrans are there, Lilith too. I have her scent…the Dotari is with them too."

"I'm right here." Gor'al waved a hand. "Can we…can we please go somewhere else?"

"Wedge formation," Hoffman said. "Movement to contact. Watch your sectors." He winced at that last command—in this dark, they could barely see a few feet ahead of them.

The lieutenant followed Steuben through the jungle until they came up to a small clearing. A junk heap that was once a massive all-terrain vehicle lay behind several light poles, illuminating an excavation site.

A massive door, silver beneath a thin coating of dirt and mud, was at the bottom of a packed-earth ramp.

Shadows—human-shaped shadows—danced against the vault door.

"That's them," Hoffman said. "No clear shot—"

A crash of breaking trees pulled his attention away as treetops fell against the last light of dusk. The noise of a wrecking machine moving through the jungle grew louder.

"It's coming right for us," Max said as he unslung his gauss rifle and readied a battery pack.

"Wait!" Hoffman made a slashing motion across his throat. "Wait, it'll go for—"

A shadow leapt out of the jungle and knocked a light pole to the ground. The Beast bit the battery pack and shook it violently from side to side, like a terrier killing a rat.

"Lock and load!" Hoffman called out.

Gunfire broke out from the vault door and a legionnaire vaulted over one side. He held up a jerry-rigged battery pack and sprinted into the jungle.

"What the hell's he doing?" King asked.

"Buying the others time," Steuben said.

Hoffman slammed a battery pack into his gauss rifle and removed a glittering silver shell from a pouch. He slid it into the breach and watched as the magnetic accelerators charged—charged so very slowly.

"Come on, come on," Hoffman said, giving his rifle a shake as if that would help.

The Beast slammed a foot against another light pole, casting a long shadow toward Hoffman's team. It reared back on its hind legs then sprang into the air.

The legionnaire screamed. Briefly.

"I'm green." Max hefted his rifle to his shoulder, eyes locked on the excavation site where the death cry had come from.

"Form a perimeter," Steuben said. "Circle, now!"

"We know where it is," Max hissed. He aimed down the gauss rifle's optics then hesitated. "Or do we?"

"Perimeter." King grabbed Garrison by the shoulder and shoved him to one side, orienting him toward the darkness.

Hoffman felt his rifle buzz—fully charged. He backtracked into the middle of the circle his Marines had formed, then craned his neck up slowly.

A shadow moved through the treetops.

"Up!" Hoffman jerked his muzzle high and fired. The quadrium round spat out in a hail of sparks. It struck a tree trunk and erupted into tendrils of lightning that lit up the night. Electricity stabbed through the Beast high in the canopy. The reek of ozone filled Hoffman's nose and every hair on his body stood on end.

The Beast fell, breaking every branch on the way down, and landed a few feet from Hoffman. Static crackled along the angles of its exoskeleton and its claws twitched in the air.

"It's…is it dead?" Booker asked from the other side

of the Beast.

"How about we make sure?" Garrison said, swinging the satchel charge off his back. "Got a time fuse for…thirty seconds?"

"You're only giving us thirty seconds to get away from a denethrite bomb?" Duke asked, his eyes wide.

"I dropped the other one!" Garrison said, his voice high and near panic.

"Hoffman, the vault," Steuben said. The door was open.

The Beast shifted against the ground.

"Set it off! Follow me!" Hoffman swung an arm toward the vault and took off running.

"Courtesy of the Terran Marine Corps!" Garrison twisted a handle on the satchel charge and tossed it beneath the Beast.

Hoffman glanced over his shoulder as he made it to the vault door, counting Marines as they ran past him and into the abyss within. King was the last man in.

The Beast struggled to rise, its limbs seeming to move independently of each other.

"Bad place to be, sir." Garrison grabbed Hoffman by the collar and yanked him back. The vault door slid shut with a hiss of metal against dirt.

The denethrite went off, slapping the vault door with a wave of overpressure. Dirt showered down in the near-total darkness.

Booker held a control pad in her hands, a wire leading from it into the wall.

"Pathfinders hacked the door," she said as she tapped a finger against the pad. "Ibarrans were in too much of a hurry to close it behind them."

There was a snap of glass and a glow stick lit up, casting sickly green light through the vault entrance. The walls were curved and covered in circles of tight alien script. King tossed the stick down the hallway, which continued into the dark. Boot prints made lines in the dust caked on the floor.

"We need to get out of this death funnel," King said. "The Ibarrans are armed…not sure if the Beast can even fit in here."

"I want to brag that the Beast is in a billion little pieces," Garrison said. "But discretion may be a bit more useful than ego here. Assume it survived?"

"Now you're modest?" Booker asked.

"I'd rather not count that chicken…especially when it could still eat me. You know what I mean. Hey, maybe we can lure it into a spaceship and then blow it out an airlock. That's a tried-and-true method," Garrison said.

"Steuben," Hoffman said, flicking the back of his hand against the Karigole's shoulder, "you have their scent?"

"I do." Steuben raised his chin toward the hallway. "There are hallways ahead."

"Power down. Switch to assault rifles," Hoffman said. "No need to have a beacon on for the Beast if it's still kicking."

Opal hefted his war hammer in both hands. "Smash Beast. Smash bad humans," the doughboy said.

"Can he finally kill them?" King asked.

"No," Opal said, shaking his head quickly. "But can smash feet. Ankles. Hands. Wrists. Ribs. Clavicle. Femur."

"We get it," Hoffman said.

Lights powered on up and down the hallway. Hoffman felt like they were walking down a spinal column as they hurried away from the vault door.

"Hate weird alien stuff," Garrison said. "Hated it on the Dotty ship, hate it now."

"I take no offense," Gor'al said. "And I second your current sentiments."

Chapter 17

Hoffman took a mirror off his belt and held it around a corner. No motion in the room beyond, but his gaze lingered over a heap of power armor on the floor.

"Clear," Hoffman said.

"That smell…" Max wrinkled his nose.

Hoffman sidestepped into the room, rifle up and ready.

"Far-side security, go." King slapped Max and Garrison on their backs and they hurried to the other side of the domed room, taking up positions near a hallway entrance on the opposite end.

Hoffman went to the power armor, a lighter version than what Strike Marines wore in the field, and colored deep blue. The Pathfinder crest was on what had been the wearer's breastplate. The smell of rotting flesh was almost too much for Hoffman to handle.

"The Beast can get in here," Steuben said.

Hoffman turned away, eyes watering from the stench. The walls of the domed room had shelves, all lined with tiny fragments of glowing porcelain.

"They were here." The Karigole went to an empty stretch of shelves. "Lilith and one that carries a scent of perfume, soap…and blood."

"Masha," Hoffman said.

"But what did they take?" King asked. "And why the hell would they come in here? For all we know, it's a cave with one entrance. If the Beast got out, the Beast can get back in."

"Pathfinders don't like the main entrance to any

archaeotech," Garrison said. "Bad habit of them being booby-trapped. Most of the time, they'll cut a control entrance the first time they enter a place…if they can do it without damaging the site. Don't look at me like I just grew a second head, Duke. I study other breach methods. That's why I'm a consummate professional."

"Then there's at least another way out," Hoffman said. "Lilith knows where it is…and we don't."

"Air," Gor'al said. "Well, if we had our sensor gear, we could check airflows for higher humidity and backtrack to where the Pathfinders can—"

"I can still track them." Steuben touched his nose. "Best to hurry. If they know another way out, they will not backtrack to the entrance to escape."

"Holy moly," Max said as he pulled a mirror back from around the corner. "Y'all got to see this."

Hoffman looked quickly around the corner and motioned for Duke to come forward. "Got some sight lines you need to cover," Hoffman told the sniper before he crouched and hurried out of the room.

The hallway opened up into a massive cavern where stalactites glowed from the ceiling and illuminated a space that could have held a battle cruiser. Blocks the size of tanks formed neat rows on the cavern floor, while a honeycomb of passageways and glass staircases made up the walls.

"I'm really glad we've got Steuben here," Booker said. "Searching through all this makes the fun on the Dotty ship easy in comparison."

Hoffman tested his weight on a glass catwalk before gingerly taking a few steps—with one hand on the railing in case it gave way.

Steuben shouldered past him. "They went this way," he said.

The glow from the stalactites flickered.

"Got a bad feeling about this," Max said.

A block on the ground twisted in place, exposing gaps.

"Charge up." Hoffman looked down the catwalk for cover and found nothing. He did not want to be on the glass when it came time to open fire. The illumination shrank, then shone bright again.

Steuben cracked a half-dozen glow sticks and flung them into the air.

"Set," Max said.

"Me too," Duke said, his rail rifle pointed to the ceiling. "But if I do a full-power shot in here and—"

"Don't. Garrison, get a—" Hoffman stopped as the stalactites faded to black. On the ground, the few glow sticks shown like sparse stars on the galaxy's edge.

A shadow flickered over a light.

"Area fire!" King shouted.

Three Marines opened up, the quadrium shells shooting down like pyrotechnics from a Roman candle.

Lightning crackled across the floor, flashing long shadows across the cavern as the Beast leapt from block to block. A tendril caught it in the head and it went down in a heap.

Hoffman's gauss rifle trembled in his hands and the battery pack fused up. He tossed the useless weapon aside as the rest of his Marines did the same.

"Ow, ow!" Garrison flung his gauss against the glass and swung another satchel charge off his back. He jammed a timer into the explosive and held it over the railing above where the Beast had collapsed.

"Wait…how high are we?" the breacher asked.

"What the hell are you waiting for?" King roared.

"It's shock-sensitive! Too much of a drop and we'll be part of the explosion," Garrison said.

"Do it." Hoffman chopped a hand toward Garrison's wrist.

The breacher shrugged, dropped the satchel charge, and took off running. Fast. Hoffman followed, remembering all the times Garrison had worn a shirt that said: "Bomb squad: If you see me running, try to keep up!" at PT.

If he ever wore it again, Hoffman swore he'd court-martial the breacher.

The Marines got to the end of the walkway to a silver wall with vertical gaps. Steuben thundered past Garrison, shoulder-checked him into a gap, then herded the rest of the Marines through, though Opal needed a kick to squeeze through.

"Cover your ears and open your mouth!" Garrison shouted.

Hoffman complied a split second before a concussion slapped against the wall, leaving his ears ringing and his inner ear off-balance. The cavern went pitch-dark.

"Team, count off," King said.

Hoffman started the count, listening as all eight

sounded off.

"Nine," a new voice said, and cold metal pressed against Hoffman's throat. A glow stick cracked on and a thick arm wrapped around his neck.

"Stand down!" the same voice said as the Marines raised their assault rifles. "Everyone stand down and we can get through all of this."

"Medvedev," Hoffman grunted as he tried to wiggle to a position with some leverage, "that you?"

The arm tightened enough to dissuade him from maneuvering.

"Yes, me and ten of my best legionnaires. All right behind me," Medvedev said.

"Lies," Steuben sneered. "There are three with you. One has a grenade with the pin gone. The other has her weapon trained on the fourth."

"Got you dead bang, asshole," Max said. "You want to let go of our LT now?"

"Crush you," Opal snarled and gripped the haft of his war hammer.

"Kill us and that grenade will turn us all into paint," Masha said from behind Hoffman. She came up to the Marine and gave him a quick pat on the head. "Why don't we all play nice? Yeah?" She held up a hand and the female legionnaire put the grenade in her palm. Masha spoke a quick command in Basque and the other woman vanished into the darkness behind them.

"The Beast isn't dead yet," Hoffman said. "We need to finish it—"

"You can't kill it," Lilith said, peeking over Masha's shoulder. "It's designed to be blown apart, hit by Xaros disintegration weapons. Any kind of abuse you can imagine, it will always reform. We can never destroy it."

"Then you might as well pop that grenade and save us some trouble," Garrison said. "Wait. No. Don't do that."

"Keep going," Masha said to Lilith.

"We can't destroy it, but we can trap it, put it back in the stasis chamber it was in for so long," the scientist said. "Before the Pathfinders…activated it."

"And then what?" Hoffman asked, still struggling to breathe with Medvedev's arm tight against his throat.

"Then you let us walk away," Masha said. "We've worked together during trying times. This constitutes grounds for a truce, doesn't it?"

Hoffman snarled.

"We'll need one of those neat little quadrium shells," Masha said as she picked up a gauss rifle, one with a missing battery pack, from the floor. "And your cooperation. After that, you can have Lilith and then we'll all go our merry ways, yes?"

"Sir, they're Ibarrans. We can't trust them," King said.

"Last best chance to take out the Beast," Masha snapped. "No reason to stay on Eridu." She slapped a leather case slung over one shoulder. "I've got the good stuff—we can thank Lilith for pointing those out. You live and you can tell Fallon and Yarrow they can finalize the evacuation. Kesaht are only three days away. Not a week like you thought."

"Lies," Hoffman said.

"Her breathing and heart rate are the same," Steuben said. "She's telling the truth."

"She's a frigging spy, Steuben," Garrison said. "Pretty sure she can lie better than most."

"If we all die here, the rest of the colony will be ripe for the Kesaht," Masha said. "So we ready to play nice together…or should I skip to the end?"

She jiggled the grenade.

"We have…a deal," Hoffman said.

Medvedev released his hold on the Strike Marine and shoved him away. The legionnaire tossed his gauss rifle to King, then a battery pack. The gunney glanced over it, his face contorted with anger.

"You son of a bitch, this is the weapon you took from me on Koen," King said.

"Too light, bad for accuracy." Medvedev shrugged.

"I've got it!" echoed down the hallway.

"Let's go." Masha picked up a glow stick and jogged away, toward the voice.

Hoffman tried to catch up to her in the narrow passage, but Medvedev elbowed him back. As the Marines hustled after the Ibarrans, Hoffman slowed until he was beside Steuben.

"The female," Steuben said, "the one with her face hidden by the mask and cross, her scent clings to Gor'al."

"How? Did you scent her from the city? Maybe she was around Gor'al—the Ibarrans have sleeper agents," Hoffman said.

"I know it from Nimrod, before we ever arrived here," Steuben said.

"Then she could be a crewman from the *Scipio*. Doesn't matter. We need to deal with the Beast first, then be ready for when the Ibarrans try and screw us."

"As you wish." Steuben pulled his lips back, revealing rows of needle-sharp teeth.

Chapter 18

Hoffman smelled the dead Pathfinders before he saw them. The alien script changed to red and pulsated as they went farther down the passageway. Hoffman recognized the place from the recording he saw when he first arrived.

Dried blood and viscera arced against a wall and he said a silent prayer for the corpse he had to step over. He was the last to enter a long room containing oval-shaped platforms hovering a few feet above the ground. Three dead bodies lay around an empty one, while his Marines stood on another.

Masha and Lilith stood behind a control panel made up of floating crystal. Medvedev was half-in, half-out of a passage farther behind them, the satchel of Qa'Resh tech over his shoulder.

The female legionnaire jumped onto the bare platform, a hunk of matte-black crystal tucked under one arm.

"Duncan didn't make it," she said.

"Is that…" Hoffman pointed at the crystal.

"Part of the Beast, yes." Masha waved him toward the other platform with his Marines. "You need to get on there. Mass has to be almost equal before they'll activate."

Hoffman put one foot on the platform when he got a glimpse of Lilith. The woman's eyes were wide and moist with tears. Masha stood close to her, one hand near the small of Lilith's back.

"King, weapon," Hoffman said, taking the gauss rifle from his sergeant and stepping back from the platform.

"Behind you!" Lilith cried.

Hoffman slapped the battery into the weapon and spun around, going to one knee.

The Beast gripped the sides of an opening high up on the near wall. Sparks spat out from its joints as half its head snapped from side to side like a bird.

"Come on, you bastard!" the legionnaire shouted and raised the hunk of crystal over her head. "This is what you want. Not him!"

A metallic hiss sounded from the Beast and it crept down the wall.

"Hit it when it's on the platform," Masha said. "But you need to get up there with the rest of them, fool!"

Lilith shook her head ever so slightly.

"Sir?" Duke hefted his sniper rifle.

Hoffman slid a quadrium shell into the breach, but the hum of the weapon in his hands told him he had several more seconds before it would be fully charged.

"Half a face and no balls!" The legionnaire stomped her foot on the platform. The Beast angled toward her and froze.

"Get ready, sir." The legionnaire crouched slightly, holding the crystal by her fingertips.

"Almost," Hoffman said.

The Beast's tails swished back and forth and Hoffman felt the battery's heat shoot up. The Beast leaped at the legionnaire, claws stretched out. She dropped the crystal and rolled to one side. The Beast landed over her, talons scraping against the platform.

Hoffman fired, unsure if the Q-shell was ready or not. The round struck the Beast in the flank…and nothing happened. The Beast gripped the missing piece of itself and red light shone from the cracks in the exoskeleton. The Beast raised a claw to shred the legionnaire.

Electricity snapped out of the Q-shell and crawled down the Beast's flank like lightning along the bottom of a storm cloud. A bolt struck the legionnaire in the leg and she screamed. Hoffman dropped the rifle and ran to the platform, grabbing her by the arm and hauling her off.

The Beast contorted as the quadrium shell ravaged its body. Static crackled around the Beast and it froze, claws gripped tight as if it were in pain.

A pale light appeared around the Beast and it froze in place. Hoffman looked back to his Marines, and they too were frozen, Garrison reaching toward them, mouth agape. Steuben held his scimitar back, ready to hurl at Masha. Opal's eyes were locked on Medvedev.

"Almost perfect." Masha stepped away from Lilith, a pistol levelled at Hoffman's face. "Almost. Just needed you to shoot from the platform and then I'd have this whole thing tied up with a bow."

"Let them go," Hoffman said.

"Now, now, let's stop being naïve," Masha said.

"The ship won't wait much longer," Medvedev

said. "We need to get out of here!"

The legionnaire groaned, crawling forward with her arms. "Captain…I can't feel my legs…help," she said, ripping her face mask off and tossing it to one side. Red hair spilled out and she looked up at Hoffman.

"Adams?" Hoffman reached for her out of instinct, remembering her as one of his Marines, not as a legionnaire.

Masha fired and the bullet struck the floor between them.

"No," Masha said. "She's not yours anymore, Hoffman. She's Ibarran. She always was. Always will be."

"Liar!" Rage grew inside Hoffman. He wanted to both strangle the spy and help Adams at the same time. "You've done something to her. She's a Strike Marine. Always faithful to the Corps. She—"

"Tell him." Masha wagged her barrel at Hoffman. "Tell him the truth. I want to see his face when he hears it."

Adams pulled herself up, leaning on one leg against the platform holding the Beast. She wiped a line of blood away from the corner of her mouth and shook her hair back.

"I am Ibarran," she said. "I fight for the Lady. For the Nation. It was always like this…I just didn't know until they freed me."

"Freed you? This is wrong, Adams. You served next to me," Hoffman said, jabbing a hand at the team trapped in stasis, "beside them, for years. You were never Ibarran!"

"Let's drive this point home," Masha said. "Legionnaire Adams, draw your sidearm and kill him."

"Are you insane!?" Medvedev shouted.

"You have your doubts too." Masha cocked her pistol up toward the ceiling. "Let's know for sure."

Adams drew a gun from a thigh holster and racked a round into the chamber.

"Adams…what have they done to you?" Hoffman asked.

Adams raised her weapon, hand trembling. "Lady Ibarra loves us," she said. "She always will. We cannot fail her."

"Belay that order," Medvedev said. "I am your commander and you will not kill him. Obey!" His last word carried an odd inflection.

Adams shook her head and lowered her weapon.

"Lieutenant, I never wanted to hurt you or the team. I'm not one of Valdar's Hammers anymore," she said.

"I'll do it myself!" Masha snapped her pistol toward Hoffman and there was a crack.

Hoffman flinched, then saw Masha in a column of pale light. Smoke flared from the weapon and a bullet held firm an inch from the muzzle. The spy's face was set with malice.

"We had a deal," Lilith said from the control panel.

"I help you get away and I stay behind, stop the bomb from going off. You've got the artifacts, just leave!"

Medvedev drew a pistol but kept it pointed to the ground. He went to Adams and picked her up. As he carried her back to the other tunnel, he kept his eyes locked on Hoffman.

"Let Masha go," he said.

"I can turn it on," Lilith said with a frown. "Turning the right ones off…not so sure. I could end up releasing the Beast, or the Marines, or all three. You want to come another couple of steps forward? I can almost get you with the last stasis emitter."

Medvedev cursed. He looked to the tunnel then back at Masha.

"Damn you, Hoffman. We're not done, you understand?" Medvedev backed into the tunnel. "This isn't over!"

He turned and disappeared into the darkness.

"Wait! Adams!" Hoffman started after them, but Lilith grabbed him by the sleeve and stopped him.

"No, just let them go," she pleaded. "I have less than an hour to save my husband, your commander. We need to get word back to the city. If you go after him, they *will* kill you."

"What did he get away with—the artifacts?" Hoffman asked. "Maybe we can stop them before they get through the Crucible."

"Doesn't matter to me." Lilith balled her fists. "We need to save my husband!"

"What about my Marines?"

"They're…just fine. Probably. I wasn't kidding about not being a hundred percent sure how to work the controls," she said.

Hoffman touched a pouch containing a radio and a separate battery. "I need…I need to get to the surface," Hoffman said. "You stay here and figure out which buttons to push."

"The Pathfinders cut a hole a few rooms that way." Lilith pointed to another tunnel. "I forgot to mention that to Masha. Bitch."

The Ibarran spy was still a statue in light.

"Don't release her until I'm back," Hoffman said.

****

Masha's gun recoiled, stopping next to her cheek. She smiled, looking for the corpse of a problematic Strike Marine. Her smile vanished, replaced by a look of confusion. Hoffman wasn't dead; he was gone.

"The hell?" She glanced at her pistol in time to see a mottled hand slap the weapon away.

Opal clasped a meaty paw against her neck and lifted her off the ground. His lips twitched as he brought her nearly nose to nose with his Neanderthal features.

"Happy…little trees," Masha gasped as she kicked meekly at the doughboy.

"Don't like you." Opal tightened his grip and Masha croaked.

"No!" Garrison shouted. "Bad, Opal! Bad! You drop that thing right now!"

Masha landed badly and went face-first into the ground when Garrison slammed a boot between her shoulder blades. Masha felt her wrists press together as someone wrapped them with cloth. She blinked hard and tried to call for Medvedev.

Garrison went prone, eye to eye with the spy.

"Well, hello there, little miss." He smiled. "Welcome back to Strike Marine custody. I've been waiting a long time for this, especially since you kicked me square in the twig and berries!"

"Funny, I didn't think I hit anything," Masha managed as her ankles were hog tied to her ankles.

"Prisoner needs to lose her speaking privileges, right, Gunney?" Garrison tapped the floor.

"Sounds about right," King said.

Garrison produced a rolled-up sock, one moist with the swamp and sweat.

"Wait!" Masha shook her head like a recalcitrant baby refusing mashed peas as Garrison tried to jam the gag into her mouth. "Wait, we can work something out!"

"You want this the easy way or do I get Opal to help?" Garrison asked.

Masha's nostrils flared and she opened her mouth. Garrison jammed the sock between her teeth and threw an empty satchel over her head.

"Oorah!" Garrison popped to his feet and mimicked firing twin pistols over the hog-tied Masha. "I take back everything bad I ever said about Eridu. This place officially rocks."

"You are overcompensating for past failures,"

Steuben said. "You were the first to obey her command to jump on the stasis platform."

"OK, we all fell for that, except for the lieutenant, which is why he's paid the big bucks," Garrison said.

"That was legitimate," Lilith said from where she sat next to the control panel as Booker examined her with a medi-gauntlet and touched bruises with a flesh knitter. "I did need a mass approximation to power up the stasis field."

"And just so you know, Mr. Karigole," Garrison said, pointing at the spy, "this one is dangerous and tricky. Don't let her bat those baby-blue eyes at you and think she's anything but an Ibarran thief and assassin. You hear that, Masha? The Terran Union's got you dead to rights."

Masha extended both her middle fingers.

"OK, that hood isn't getting the job done." Garrison shook his head.

"Marines," Hoffman said as he bounded down the

ramp, "extraction's coming. Everyone to the surface."

"My husband? The bomb?" Lilith stood up.

"They evacced headquarters before it could go off," Hoffman said. "It's been neutralized."

"We going after Medvedev?" Max hefted his assault rifle. "I owe him."

"*Scipio*'s watching for their ship, but there's a lot of sky to cover," Hoffman said. "Get the prisoner to the surface and keep a perimeter up. The Ibarrans might come back for this one."

"Hope they do." Max slid a fused gauss rifle beneath Masha's bonds and lifted her up.

"Let's convince her Steuben will cook her for dinner," Garrison said. "Karigole do that, right?"

"Is there a wedding?" Steuben asked as they went up the ramp.

Hoffman signaled for King to fall back then waited until there was space between them and the rest of the team.

"Sir?"

"One of the legionnaires…it was Adams," Hoffman said and King missed a step. "Saw with my own eyes. No mistake it was her. It all makes sense now. The sudden transfer, why the intelligence officers were so interested in her…the Ibarrans must have brought her to Eridu since she was embedded in the Terran Union for so long."

"By the Saint…how? How was a traitor under our nose the whole time?" King asked.

"Hell if I know," Hoffman said. "Chalk it up to another failure on my part. I lost Masha not once but twice, and she murdered people on Mars when Adams and other traitors broke out of prison. Then the *Breitenfeld* gets captured while we were her onboard contingent."

"We weren't onboard when that happened," King said.

"We should've been there to protect our ship. Save

Admiral Valdar. Now the Ibarrans will probably get away with whatever Medvedev had in that pack…and with Adams. Screwed it all up again, didn't I?"

"Stop." King grabbed the lieutenant by the shoulder and pointed back to the chamber with the Beast. "You stopped that damn thing. The colony will get evacced now, hundreds of lives saved because you were on the ball. We've got Masha. Alive. And when the intelligence types get ahold of her, she'll give up everything she knows about what the Ibarrans are up to in the Union. Today is a win, sir. Not total victory, but we—you—made it happen. As for Adams…the Strike Marines never forget their own. We'll track her down. I never thought I'd see Masha again, but the Lord works in mysterious ways."

"We are *not* transferring custody of that spy to anyone on this planet," Hoffman said. "Not making that mistake again."

"Roger that." King nodded. "We've got that score

settled. Now we need to find Valdar and the *Breitenfeld*, bring them home."

Hoffman touched his earbud. "Mule's almost here. Double time."

Chapter 19

Hoffman and King charged up the ramp of an idling Mule transport. The craft lifted off before they made it into the cargo bay. Crewmen directed them toward Colonel Fallon and Yarrow at the forward end of the bay, where the latter embraced his wife and the two spoke rapid-fire in a language that Hoffman assumed was Akkadian.

Dr. Masako sat at the far end of the benches, a duffle bag on either side of her.

"I got the skinny." Fallon glanced at Masha, pinned to the deck by Opal's foot.

"Beast is neutralized," Hoffman said. "I don't know

if it's even possible to destroy it."

"Construction teams will bury the lab at first light, then the planet will be evacced completely," Fallon said.

"The Ibarran said the Kesaht were days away?"

"She said that." Hoffman shrugged. "Doesn't necessarily mean we should believe her."

"No chances; fleet's already mobilizing transports." Fallon breathed a sigh of relief. "Wish I could offer you and your Marines more than an 'attaboy' right now. We've been reassigned back to 14th Fleet. The attack on the Kesaht's home world is still a go and they need every hand on deck for this one. Biggest assault the Union's put together since the Ember War."

"Sir," Hoffman's mind spun between disbelief and outrage, "what about Valdar and his ship? The crew? Masha must know where the Ibarrans have—"

"Ibarrans aren't invading our colonies. Kesaht are. High Command wants to end the war with the aliens with one swift stroke. Then we've got a host of other problems before we can get to the Ibarrans," Fallon said. "It's bad, Lieutenant. Last time I remember it being worse was when the *Midway* came back and we realized just how unprepared we were for the Xaros siege. Need you and your Marines to find your iron."

Hoffman quelled his doubts. This wasn't the time to crack—not when his team would follow his every mood. If he stayed strong, they would stay stronger.

"Aye aye," Hoffman said.

"We're dropping the Yarrows, then we're making straight for the *Scipio*, then the 14th Fleet anchorage," Fallon said. "I'm going to have a word with the prisoner."

"I'll keep our Marines' heads on straight," King said. "Get the REMFs back in the city to have our power armor waiting for us."

"Good." Hoffman went over to an open space on the bench next to Masako, his mind in a haze. He sat hard and rubbed away a growing headache.

"You look like a can of smashed assholes," Masako said. "But you did pretty good…for a crunchy."

"What are you doing here?" Hoffman asked, one eye on King as he spoke to the team, their faces growing longer by the second.

"You ever heard of an orbital assault that didn't take casualties? I asked for reassignment to a combat hospital. I'm not a board-certified trauma surgeon, but I'm value-added in the operating room. Besides, I'm sick of backwater and safe assignments." She raised her braced arm and flexed her fingers. "Bad enough I washed out of armor. I'm not going to finish the war shoveling manure in Louisiana."

"Is that…Patton?"

"Brains and brawn." She winked at him. "Do me a favor, don't get dragged into my OR on a gurney. Don't want to see you in a professional manner. Got it?"

"I can promise, but it won't be up to me if I end up lying," Hoffman said.

"You got that big doughboy to take care of you."

"We take care of each other. Always have and always will."

Masako patted the duffle between them. "Want some shut-eye?"

"You see my Marines sleeping?" Hoffman stood up, feeling aches and pains growing down his back and his legs.

He went to the loose circle his team had formed around King. Gor'al, Opal, and Steuben made for unusual additions to Valdar's Hammers, but he wouldn't trade them out for anyone.

"It true, sir?" Max asked. "We're going to the main event?"

"We are. Don't have much else in the way of details," Hoffman said.

"So much for my plans to help out with Masha's interrogation in Hawaii," Garrison said, catching more than one raised eyebrow from his team. "What? A guy can hope, can't he?"

"We need equipment and an operation plan," Steuben said.

"Why?" Duke spat into a plastic bottle. "We didn't have either and look how well we did back there."

"Is that more Earth humor?" Steuben asked.

"It is." Hoffman rubbed the bridge of his nose. "No rest for us this time, Hammers. Steuben, you still with us?"

"If you are going to kill Kesaht, then I will fight beside you until the last of them lie dead at my feet," the Karigole said.

"I am not sharing a foxhole with him," Garrison mumbled.

"If the Dotari Marines recall me," Gor'al said as his quills bristled, "I will pretend a dog ate the message. That is an acceptable excuse for humans, yes?"

"Then we're together." Hoffman looked at Opal.

"Opal with sir. Always."

"Always."

Epilogue

Medvedev stood in a small room, his hands clasped behind his back, the satchel over one shoulder. Adams was behind him, one foot in a polymer cast.

"I hear them coming." Medvedev turned his head to look over his shoulder. "Remember what to do. What I told you."

"Of course, sir, but if I hadn't—"

"That's enough, Legionnaire. I was in command and that is the end of it."

Doors slid open and two hulking guards in ornate armor and polearms filled the doorway. Medvedev and

Adams went to one knee, right forearm braced over their thigh, the other fist to the ground. Cold crept into the room and Medvedev cast his eyes downward.

Frost bit into his ears and jawline as a pair of silver feet beneath a gray robe entered his field of view.

"You return," Stacey Ibarra said. "But you return…missing something. Someone. Someone I needed."

"The Akkadian Lilith still lives, my Lady," Medvedev said. "The Terran Union is evacuating Eridu as we speak."

A metal hand carved into a perfect facsimile of a woman's reached under Medvedev's chin but stopped short of touching him.

"Look at me, warrior," Stacey said.

Medvedev lifted his gaze and tears froze in his eyes as he saw Stacey Ibarra's perfect—but still—face clad in silver.

"You did not return with the Akkadian." The words

came, but her mouth did not move.

"No, my Lady. I have failed you." Medvedev tried to look away, but a touch from a freezing fingertip kept his eyes up. "I cannot be forgiven."

"It is my fault, my Lady," Adams said. "I…hesitated when ordered to kill a Union Marine."

"Adams," Stacey said.

"You know me?"

"I know all my children. You were rescued from the gallows on Mars. Once a Strike Marine. The one you didn't kill…you were close to him?"

"Once my team leader, yes, my Lady."

"The order was wrong," Medvedev said. "The Marine was honorable, had helped us defeat the Beast and saved all our lives. I countermanded the order. Had I not done that, Legionnaire Adams would have done as Masha wanted. Adams is of the Nation. She is true."

"I believe you," Stacey Ibarra said. "Would killing

that Marine have changed the mission?"

"No, my Lady," Medvedev said. "The Akkadian was treacherous. There was no way I could stop her from capturing Masha. I chose to abort, return with what I could."

"And what did you bring me?" Stacey moved her hand from his chin to the satchel. A globe glowed within and floated out, levitating just over her fingertips, humming as a golden lattice formed around it.

"My, my…this is special," Stacey said. "An ignition device. I can use this. Yes, the mission was not a total loss."

"And a copy of the Akkadian archives." Medvedev held up a data drive from the satchel. "Masha gathered all she could."

"She died?" Stacey took the drive and her fingers molded into the access ports. Screens flashed across her exposed shell.

"Lesser Strike Marines would have killed her," Medvedev said. "I believe Hoffman too honorable for that. Masha is a prisoner of war. The Union will murder her simply for existing."

"And they will pay for that death a hundredfold," Stacey said. "But Masha sent back some of what I needed. It seems the final task is at hand, and I must do it myself. Do you believe in fate, Medvedev?"

"I believe in you, my Lady."

"And I in you, my child. You're reassigned. I have something special in mind for you. Adams…will return to the Legions."

Stacey left and heat slowly seeped back into Medvedev's flesh.

Adams sniffed and wiped a sleeve across her eyes.

"I didn't…I didn't think she'd be like that," Adams said. "So beautiful. So perfect."

"She loves us," Medvedev said. "We cannot fail her

again."

"If I'd shot Hoffman, we would have the Akkadian here for the Lady, wouldn't we?" she asked.

"I doubt that. Hoffman would have honored the deal, you know that. You know him."

"The deal was not for us to leave with the Akkadian. Masha was playing him along, and he fell for it. I failed the mission. Next time, I will not hesitate," said the former Strike Marine. "If I must, I will kill Hoffman and all the rest of them. For the Lady. For our Nation."

"For us all."

THE END

The series concludes in GOTT MIT UNS, coming early 2019!

FROM THE AUTHORS

Hello Dear and Gentle Reader,

Thank you for reading The Beast of Eridu. We hope you enjoyed Lieutenant Hoffman and his team's adventure, much more on the way!

Please leave a review on Amazon and let us know how we've done as storytellers, you're feedback is important to us.

Drop us a line at Richard@richardfoxauthor.com and scottmoonwritesanovel@gmail.com.

Also By Richard Fox:

The Ember War Saga:
1. The Ember War
2. The Ruins of Anthalas
3. Blood of Heroes
4. Earth Defiant
5. The Gardens of Nibiru
6. The Battle of the Void
7. The Siege of Earth
8. The Crucible
9. The Xaros Reckoning

Terran Armor Corps:

1. Iron Dragoons
2. The Ibarra Sanction
3. The True Measure
4. A House Divided
5. The Last Aeon
6. Ferrum Corde (Coming late 2018!)

Terra Nova Chronicles

1. Terra Nova
2. Bloodlines
3. Redemption's Shadow (Coming early 2019!)

The Exiled Fleet Series:

1. Albion Lost
2. The Long March
3. Their Finest Hour (Coming early 2019!)

About Scott Moon

Scott Moon has been writing fantasy and science fiction for over thirty-six years. When not reading, writing, or spending time with his awesome family, he enjoys playing the guitar, Brazilian Jiu Jitsu, and watching movies. Dog guy. Fan of the military. A career law enforcement officer, he served on the SWAT team, Gang Unit, Exploited Missing Child Unit, and helped catch a serial killer. He is also a co-host of the popular Keystroke Mcdium show (www.KeyStrokeMedium.com)

More Books and Stories by Scott Moon

The Chronicles of Kin Roland

Enemy of Man
Son of Orlan
Weapons of Earth

Read the entire Chronicles of Kin Roland trilogy on Kindle Unlimited!

SMC Marauders
Bayonet Dawn

Burning Sun

Son of a Dragonslayer
Dragon Badge
Dragon Attack
Dragon Land

The Fall of Promisdale
Death by Werewolf

Grendel Uprising

Proof of Death
Blood Royal
Grendel

Darklanding
Episode 1: Assignment Darklanding
Episode 2: Ike Shot the Sheriff
Episode 3: Outlaws
Episode 4: Runaway
(A new episode of Darklanding will be published every 18 days!)

Please visit http://www.ScottMoonWriter.com for more information.

Join the Scott Moon Group on Facebook to talk about books and stuff:
https://www.facebook.com/groups/ScottMoonGroup/

Printed in Great Britain
by Amazon